IT IS WHAT IT IS

By:

Brenda Stokes Lee

And

Manswell T. Peterson

Contents

It Is What It Is

Chapter 1

Chapter 2

Chapter 3

Chapter 4

Chapter 5

Chapter 6

Chapter 7

Chapter 8

Chapter 9

Chapter 10

Chapter 11

Chapter 12

Chapter 13

Chapter 14

Chapter 15

Chapter 16

Chapter 17

Chapter 18

Chapter 19

Chapter 20

Chapter 21

Chapter 22

Chapter 23

Chapter 24

Chapter 25

Chapter 26

Chapter 27

Chapter 28

Chapter 29

Chapter 30

About Author Brenda Stokes Lee

Contact Brenda

About Author Manswell T. Peterson

Contact Manswell

CHAPTER 1

Mykal Roman took one final look at his Miami home. Boxes were stacked neatly waiting for the movers to load them in the Pod shipper and ship them to Atlanta the following morning. He sighed deeply, as he remembered the fantastic times he had in Miami. Now it was off to Atlanta, where his dream of owning his own limo company would finally become a reality.

A devilish smile tugged at the corners of his sexy mouth as he considered the amazing woman who dared him to dream it was possible, Victoria Dickerson. His dick stiffened at just the thought of her name.

Mykal chuckled, "Victoria Dickerson, woman you are one hell of a ride. I'll miss you most of all."

"Sure, that's what you say now. I bet you'll have some pretty blonde on her knees, sucking this big, hard mahogany dick within one hour after you land at Hartsfield- Jackson Atlanta International Airport. Hell, you'll probably find some horny little stewardess to do it for you before you even land." Victoria whined as she hugged his waist from the rear and coyly slid her hands along the front of his slacks. "Oh, Rome why do you have to go? Why can't you just start your business, here in Florida?"

Mykal did not answer her immediately. Victoria's nimble, long fingers had worked his zipper and relieved his large, swollen manhood from the restraints of his pants. It was hard, it was menacing and it wanted a taste of pussy. His eyes closed slowly as her soft hand slowly traveled up and down the length of his very impressive dick. It felt wonderful and Mykal had to admit that he hated leaving her behind.

Now, Victoria and Mykal loved each other, but they were not what you would call in love. In fact, they weren't even a couple. They were very good friends with extremely rewarding benefits. Victoria was a free spirit who refused to be tied down or control by any man, not even her insanely rich husband Richard Dickerson, or Tricky Dick as Mykal often referred to him.

Victoria met Mykal five years earlier and fell head over ass in love with his ten and a half inch rock solid, always hard dick. Their brief one night affair turned into a mutually beneficial friendship that they both enjoyed to this very day. She never promised Mykal more than an eager pussy and a hungry mouth and he never wanted it.

Victoria was slightly older than Mykal, had married twice for money and as far as he knew didn't have any kids and didn't want any. Mykal, who was now thirty two, was tired of chasing tail. His friends with benefits relationship with Victoria had allowed him to virtually OD on Miami pussy. He was sick of the chase and just wanted to be called, dad.

Victoria neither shared his values or his dreams of starting a family. Mykal knew that even if he managed to convince Victoria to leave her rich husband and move to Atlanta with him it would never work. Mykal was ready to start a family and Victoria was just ready to start a party. Nothing about her screamed soccer mom and that was what Mykal was looking for.

Like it or not, the handsome young bachelor had to admit that his biological clock was ticking loud and fast. Mykal longed for a son and a daughter and he was prepared to give up his hoeing ways to get them. Unfortunately, he couldn't do that in Miami.

Mykal had blown through a small arena of Miami women and there was nowhere he could go were his name and reputation did not preceded him. Sadly, his time in Miami was officially up. It was time to shred his pro-players card and allow himself to fall in love for the first time in his life.

Mykal loved Victoria, she was good to him and brought him any and everything his heart fancied. He just wasn't in love with her. She was one of his best friends, but that was far as it went. Somewhere in her thirty nine years of life, Victoria had been damaged and Mykal instinctively knew he didn't have the time or the patience to repair her. Besides, she was already on rich husband number two and travelling two hundred miles and hours headed to divorce court. Mykal would be damned if he was number three.

"So, you're not going to answer me?" Victoria asked as she slid around to the front of him and squatted before him as she continued to slowly stroke his veiny manhood.

"Woman you know I can't even remember my name when you're handling my dick." He groaned as he watched her work.

Victoria's position revealed she wasn't wearing panties beneath her short, form fitting black dress. Her pussy glistened with her juices and invited Mykal's touch, he didn't decline the invitation. His thick fingers slid along her tight wet slit before disappearing between the plump lips of her shaved mound.

A snake like hiss escaped Victoria's lips as Mykal's slow hand pleasured her. Her big hazel eyes met his briefly before rolling to the back of her head like tiger eye marbles. Mykal smiled as he marveled how exceptionally beautiful Victoria was.

Extraordinarily long, loosely curled blonde highlighted hair frame her attractive, tanned face. Big expressive, doe like eyes, thin, but seductive lips and a pointed, upturned nose blended seamlessly to create the face of this stunning white woman. Although she was almost forty, Victoria was well preserved and possessed a natural body that would make any twenty five year old woman run to the gym to step up their game.

Sensational, perky full breast, a gift from her first husband and a perfect round onion booty, a gift from her second husband where put to shame by her rock hard six pac abs.

Victoria worshipped her body like it was a shrine and she lived at the gym. Training with two of Miami's best fitness trainers, Victoria refused to grow old gracefully. She was in peak health and easily mistaken to be in her mid- twenties.

"Tell me you're going to miss this." She pleaded after licking the bead of pre-cum which had formed at the tip of Mykal's throbbing manhood.

Compassion for her plight touched Mykal. It was no secret that he was Victoria's only real friend. He hated to leave her, but he had to go, destiny had wrapped a tight noose around his neck and was pulling him to Atlanta. Naturally, he'd miss her, they were good friends and phenomenal lovers.

"Tori, you already know the answer to that question." He sighed.

"Maybe, but I need to hear the words from your mouth. I need to know for certain that I was more to you than warm pussy."

"Yes! Hell yes! I'm going to miss the hell out of you. We've shared some incredible times... Both in and out of bed. You're my friend, and I'll never forget you. It's just that life has brought us to a fork in the road. I have to go one way and you have to go the other. Okay?"

Victoria discreetly wiped away the lone tear that had quickly formed in the corner of her eye. She understood that Mykal was at a point in his life where he needed more than amazing sex to feel like a man. He was childless and he needed a wife and children to fill that massive void that had formed in his spirit. It hurt to realize that she was incapable of fulfilling that need for him. That ship had sailed for Victoria and she wasn't trying to catch a ride on it anyway. She was done with marriage, two bad marriages were two too many.

"Tori, please don't." Mykal begged as he caught her tearing up.

"I can't help it. I just know I'm going to be miserable without you and the thought of it breaks my heart.

Mykal, had never once seen Victoria, or Tori as he called her cry. She was a strong, sophisticated, Pit-bull of a woman. He knew she was hurting and he knew why. Fortunately, he knew how to ease the pain for at least a few hours.

He said not another word as he lifted her body from the floor and passionately kissed her. Their tongues wrestled for dominance as her legs wrapped around his torso. Grabbing her by her firm ass Mykal lifted her high until her wet pussy was level with his mouth. Like a ravenous wolf he attacked it as her back slammed against the living-room wall.

Victoria clutched his head as he devoured her hot pussy pie one lick at a time. All of her trouble immediately dissipated as Mykal's tongue stroked the inner walls of her slick pussy. Gyrating hard against his mouth she doubled her pleasure as she rode his face. Squeals of pleasure and delight filled the room as her Category- 6 orgasm threatened to annihilate her completely.

Her head thrashed violently, whipping her long hair wildly making her look like a sex crazed Medusa. Her grip on the back of his head tightened and Mykal knew she was a clit lick away from a core meltdown. Sucking her cherry red clit as far in his mouth as it would go without ripping from her body, he gave her the relief she sought.

A split second later, Victoria lost all control and her body convulsed with a Tsunami of perfect pleasure. Screaming loudly she squirted her sticky nectar in Mykal's mouth as he continued to insatiably lap at her quivering sex. Satisfied that she was satisfied he maneuvered her over his monstrous dick and impelled her with it repeatedly.

Semi-comatose at this point Victoria laced her arms around Mykal's neck as he slammed his body against hers, going balls to ass deep with each and every thrust. A little shy of twenty pumps later he shot his hot sticky load deep within her.

They stared eye to eye as the last few squirts coated her walls. His eyes told her everything she needed to know. Mykal loved her in his own way, but he needed more. Sucking his tongue in her mouth Victoria savored her last taste of Mykal Roman, or Rome as she fondly nicknamed him.

After a night of wild, unbridled leg numbing sex, Victoria was finally prepared to release him.

CHAPTER 2

Victoria walked into her multi-million dollar Atlanta mansion to find her husband, Richard Dickerson, waiting for in his study. It was five in the morning and he was thoroughly pissed. Tale- tale signs of alcohol on his breath and on the end table next to him clued Victoria in that he'd been drinking all night.

Actually, she really didn't need any clues. Richard was a flirtatious old drunk. Victoria knew it when she married him. It was no secret to anyone, including Richard that she didn't really love him and only married him for his money. Richard wanted a beautiful trophy wife to show off to his colleagues at the Country Club and Victoria... Well, let's just say that Victoria wanted a man who could treat her to the finer things in life and enhance her financial portfolio by at least ten million easy dollars.

Already independently wealthy from the settlement of her divorce from a Superstar NBA player, Victoria really didn't need to remarry. She certainly didn't need the money as she was awarded an obscene amount of alimony, because her first husband was a serial cheater. Nonetheless, she agreed to marry

Richard because she liked him and he promised her a healthy settlement if they should ever divorce.

Sex between them was basically, non- existent as Richard was a Down- Low male hoe who loved eighteen year old boys. So, Victoria never once was asked to fulfill her wifely duties. She got all she needed and more from Mykal, so that was perfectly fine with her. Yes, their marriage was a sham and Victoria was merely a front to hide Richard's homosexual life style from his overbearing, filthy rich mother. Afraid she'd cut him out of her will, Richard begged Victoria to marry him so his mother wouldn't suspect he was gay.

Handsome in his own right, the forty five year old was considered one of the most sought after bachelors and in Atlanta when they married. The reality of the situation was that Richard was a sloppy drunk who struggled with his homosexuality and mommy issues.

Victoria knew what she was getting in when she accepted his proposal. Naturally, Mother Dearest insisted upon and iron clad pre-nuptial agreement, which Victoria gracefully signed. Little did Psycho Mom know that Richard had deposited twenty million dollars in an account for Victoria securing her future and her silence.

Uncharacteristically pissy drunk, Richard pounced on her the second she walked through the door. "Well, well, well! Look who finally decided to bring their whoring ass home!" He slurred as he took another swig of his aged Scotch right from the bottle.

Victoria ignored him, she knew how he was when he got drunk, a classless ass. Slipping her designer stilettos off, she headed for her sitting room. Richard followed on her heels dressed only in silk boxer shorts. He reeked of piss and Victoria knew he had somehow found rock bottom, yet had not discover the bottom of his bottle.

"Hi, dear. I see you've been drinking. Why don't you put the bottle down and let me get you some coffee?"

"What?" He slurred as he stumbled into her study and plopped in a chair. "Did I ask you for some fucking coffee? Yes! I'm drunk, but that's not the issue."

Victoria took a seat at her desk and opened her laptop. Ignoring the fact that his pissy ass was sitting on her expensive, white Victorian antique love seat, she started pressing keys. "Oh yeah? So what exactly is the problem this time my love?" She asked as she typed in Richard's username and password to his online banking account. He used the same password for everything and Victoria knew it. It was easy to remember- DickLovesDick! "What a fucking idiot!" She mumbled beneath her breath as his account information popped up.

"So, where were you all night? You think you can just come and go all hours of the night as you please. Huh?"

"Yeah, pretty much. We agreed on that point before we were married. My personal life is my personal life, just as your personal life is yours. I don't ask you whose dick you suck and you don't ask me whose dick I suck. It's in the pre-nupt, remember?" Victoria calmly stated as she examined Richard's bank statement.

"Oh, I know whose dick you were sucking. I don't have to ask, the same dick you been swinging on like a great white ape from the first day I met you."

Victoria could feel her cheeks flush with anger. She suppressed the urge to jump across her desk and knock his bitch ass the fuck out. Instead she chilled. "Dick let me get you something to eat. Did you eat anything?"

"I'm not hungry... I'm thirsty. And stop trying to change the fucking subject!" Richard retorted as he took another gulp of alcohol. Victoria did not respond. She had never seen him so agitated. "You were with that black nigger of yours weren't you?"

The vulgarity of what Richard said cut Victoria to her core. Chills shot up her spine as the "N" word leaped out of her husband's mouth and hung in the air like the stench of rhinoceros shit.

"Wow! That's a new word for you. When did you add that to your vulgar vocabulary?" She sarcastically responded.

"When that nigger started fucking my wife!" He snapped back in defiance. "What you don't like it?"

"No actually I don't. That's the most vial word anyone can call anyone else and if it comes out of your mouth one more time there will be consequences and repercussions. Translation say it one more time and I will FUCK your drunk ass up!" She snarled as her eyes locked on him and dared him to utter a syllable that even begin with the letter N. "That word is offensive, and socially unacceptable and I will not allow you or anyone else to use it in my house."

"Your house? You mean my house!" He chuckled.

"No Bitch! I meant what I said. This is my house. You brought it for me, my name is on the deed, which makes it my house. Now say the N word in my damn house again and see if I don't kick your fucking ass!" She screamed back.

"Wow aren't you the defensive one. Last I checked you were white! It's not like I called you one. Anyway... That's not the point."

Victoria stared at her pissy drunk husband of three years. She bit her bottom lip, sighed deeply and considered her options. She realized she didn't have any. The only person in Miami who even liked her, let alone loved her was on a plane to Atlanta. It was at that moment she came to the chilling conclusion that her sham of a marriage was officially over.

She also made the executive decision to create her own severance package. Victoria noticed that this particular account had a little over twelve million dollars in savings. Transferring ten million to her personal expense account she continued to pretend she was interested in resolving her problems with Richard.

"So what is the point love? Exactly what is all this nonsense about? Dick you're not a racist, what's going on with you?" She asked as she confirmed the wire transfer with Richard's secret, safety passcode- *DickLuvs2SuckBigA$$Dicks!!*

It was a very large transfer and every safety precaution had to be taken, so it was no surprise to Victoria when their home phone immediately rang. It was the bank.

"Hello, Dickerson's resident. Victoria speaking."

"Hi, this is Mrs. Stewart from Chase Manhattan Bank, sorry to disturb you, but we have to verify a wire transaction. Is this Mrs. Victoria Dickerson?"

"Yes, it's me. How can I help you?" Placing her palm over the receiver of the phone Victoria mouthed, "It's Citibank. I moved some money around. I hope you don't mind. I think she wants you. What should I say?"

"Vicky, I'm drunk. I can't talk to her right now. Just tell her to give you whatever you want." He waved her off. "I don't care, tell her it's fine."

"Mrs. Dickerson is your husband home?"

"Yes, do you need to speak to him?"

"Yes, I need him to verbally authorize the bank transfer into your account."

"Understandable. Let me see if I can get him on the phone." Victoria put her on speaker phone. "Okay, he's here, Mrs. Stewart."

"Hi, Mr. Dickerson, this is Mrs. Stewart from Citibank. I need to confirm a wire transfer you made to your wife's account."

"Yes, I can confirm the transfer." Richard responded in a sober voice.

"Sir, are you aware of the amount of this transfer?"

"What's your name?" He asked, irritated as his buzz quickly faded leaving him with a pounding headache.

"Mrs. Stewart... My name is Mrs. Stewart. As I was saying…"

"Mrs. Stewart, are you aware that it's five thirty in the morning. Naturally, I'm aware of the transferred amount. I made the transfer. Now is there anything else I can do for you before I hang up?" Richard quickly cut her off.

"Sorry, to disturb you sir. My apologies. We're just trying to protect your money. Please enter your safety lock code and I'll make the transfer immediately."

"No problem. Sorry, to be rude but my wife and I were in the middle of something when you called." He apologized.

"No problem Mr. Dickerson, I understand. Please enter your safety lock code and we'll be finished."

"Okay." Richard responded as he entered his safety lock code- *DickLuvs2SuckBigA$$Dicks!!*

"Okay well that will do it." Mrs. Stewart responded. "The sum of ten…."

The crafty Victoria quickly turned off the speaker phone before Richard could hear the amount. "Okay, thank you, Mrs. Stewart."

"You're welcome, Mrs. Dickerson. Sorry about the disturbance Mr. Dickerson."

Victoria quickly switched back to speaker phone. "It's no problem, right dear?"

"No problem. Thanks Mrs. Stewart. Sorry about my rudeness, as I said you caught me at a bad time." Richard replied.

"Thanks for choosing Citibank. Have a good day." Mrs. Stewart responded before hanging up.

Victoria slyly sighed a slow sigh of relief. "Okay, so what's got you all hyped up? This is so out of character for you."

Dick drew in a long deep breath and then sighed deeply. "You're right Vicky, I'm sorry. What I said was insensitive, ignorant and plain wrong. I'm sorry I offended you. I'll make a donation to a charity or something, next week."

"Okay, well I guess that's a start, but I meant what I said, Dick. I will not hesitate to slap that word out of your mouth the next time I hear it. Are we clear?" Victoria assured him as she watched ten million dollars be wired from his bank to her bank. A devious smile transformed her pretty face as the message- *"Transfer completed,"* flashed on the screen.

"Yeah, we're clear. Vicky, that's not me and you know it. It's just that Mother thinks…"

"Let me stop you right there, because you of all people know that I don't give a flying flea fuck what Catherine Dickerson thinks."

"I know, I know, but I have to agree with her on this one."

"Okay, so what does Mother think?"

Richard hesitated and considered his words. "There's no easy way to say this."

"Yeah, there is! Just open your mouth and say it." Victoria challenged.

"Okay, here goes… Mother thinks it's time we start a family. I'm her only son and she wants grandchildren."

Victoria stared at Richard like he was a unicorn that had sprouted a bright purple dick where his horn should be. "You and your mama both lost your damn minds if you think I'm going to ruin my body having a baby for you two snobs to ruin. Oh fuck that bullshit!"

"Just hear me out Vicky…"

"Are you kidding me? Dick, you can't possibly be serious. This is not what we agreed on!"

"I know, but… Look Vicky, I want a child. I thought eventually I could convince you to…"

"To do what Dick? Huh? Convince me to allow you to fuck me! Oh hell no! Forget it because it's not going to happen. You two bitches are as crazy as Fruit Loops with buttermilk if you think I'm going to let you knock me up!"

"I'll pay you! I'll pay you ten million dollars if you'll have my child. Please, Vicky?"

"Hell, no! You couldn't give me fifty million to get pregnant by you."

"Vicky please… Will you please at least consider it?" Richard begged. "Just sleep on it! You won't even have to sleep with me, if you don't want to. We'll get a fertility specialist. Okay? Just think about it for a few days. Please?"

"Okay, but I'm not promising anything." Victoria reluctantly agreed to end the discussion, although she knew in her heart that her superficial marriage to Richard Dickerson had reached its expiration date.

Victoria packed her things and flew to Atlanta the following day.

CHAPTER 3

Suniya Simmons was exhausted when she pulled in front of her modest, contemporary Atlanta home. She had worked from sun up to sunset getting her upscale male clothing boutique ready for its grand opening. She had always dreamed of opening a store that catered to the professionally dress man with a discerning taste for cutting edge fashion. A fashion designer by nature and a former buyer for Saks, Suniya had the talent, connections and expertise to pull it off. Unfortunately, she didn't have the money. Against her better judgment she turned to her mother for a no interest, generous loan to make her dream a reality.

Suniya and her mother had a long history of resentment and disappointment between them. Barely sixteen years older than Suniya, her mother was a baby herself when her daughter was born. Understandably, she wasn't the model mother and depended on her mom, Suniya's grandmother, to step in as mom.

Unfortunately, this created an unexpected riff in their mother daughter dynamics. Suniya grew up with the preconceived notion that her mother was her sister. It wasn't until her grandmother passed that her mother told her the truth at twenty years of age. Needless to say Suniya was hurt and betrayed and absolutely refused to accept it. She immediately cut off ties with her mom and took up permanent residence in Atlanta where she attended college.

Five years had passed since that time. Many things had changed since then. Suniya had a larger than life dream and her mom had a silk multi-million dollar purse. There was just one stipulation, Suniya had to extend an olive branch of friendship to repair their torn relationship. Fortunately, mother and daughter were finally in a position where mending fences and building bridges were possible.

As Suniya gathered her things to go in the house her phone rang. It was here mother. She answered, "Hello!"

"Hey Boots, what are you doing?"

"Hey Sissy, I'm just pulling in. What are you up to?"

"Moving."

"Again?" Suniya laughed. "Sissy, what did you do?"

"Me?" She burst into laughter. "I didn't do anything. When it's over it's over."

"Are you okay?"

"Yeah! I'm better than okay. Don't worry about me I'm happy. When you leave a marriage with peace of mind you have it all. However... When you leave with a healthy alimony settlement... Well, you know what I mean."

Suniya giggled. "No, actually I don't. I've never been married and when I get married I want to be married forever. So, no... I have no concept of what you're talking about. Happy you came out ahead in the divorce, but I just want a good faithful husband that can withstand the test of time."

"God, I pray you find one. So, what is my future son in-law up to? Dare, I even ask?"

"Hopefully getting a job. I told him that he could at least pretend he wants to work."

"Boots, you're too beautiful of a woman to be settling for bullshit. Don't settle for the first man that can make your toes curl. Life's about a hell of a lot more than dick. There are two type of people on the planet, male and females. The males all have dicks. Now, your task is to find one with a dick that can put a crack in your back and a dent in the damn mortgage."

"Sissy!"

"What? I'm just being honest! Gone are the days of fucking for free! Rich men fuck as hard as broke ones… Trust me, I know! I'm a witness! So, kick his freeloading, bad credit, no job, ten baby mama having ass out and find a real man. One who is willing to take on the responsibility of providing for his woman and one day his family."

"I hear you but…"

"No! No buts Boots! Enough is enough... Can you really see yourself married to this man? Has he even entertained the concept of marrying you?"

"Sissy, I understand you're concerned about my well-being, but I have this. Okay?"

There was an uncomfortable silence. "You're right and I'm wrong. You're a woman now. You're twenty five years old, which means you're old enough to fight your own battles and make your own mistakes. If you're happy then I'm happy."

Suniya sighed before responding. She knew she had hurt her mom's feelings, but it wasn't intentional. They had come a very long way in repairing their relationship, but she still wasn't at the point where she honestly could take her mother's motherly advice. The wounds of their past was still too fresh and frankly it was too late in the game for her mother to grow up and start giving motherly advice.

"Thanks for understanding Sissy. I'm not trying to be disrespectful... It's just that..." Suniya tried to apologize.

"Nonsense. It wasn't disrespectful. You're right. This is your relationship so, it's your decision. I'll support you whatever you do... You know that right?"

"Yeah... I do. Thanks! Look, I'm exhausted, so I'm going to get in here and cook some dinner, take a shower and go to bed. I love you Sissy. Thanks for everything. I couldn't have done this without you."

"No problem. I'm happy I had the resources to bring your dream to fruition. Love you too, Boots."

Suniya smiled. Her mom was the only one left on the planet that called her Boots. It was a nickname she earned when she was five years old. Her mom brought her a pair of hot pink rain boots and Suniya refused to wear any other shoe from the moment she put them on. Rain, sleet, snow or hail, Suniya had those God awful shiny pink boots on. She even wore them to church. Her grandmother was at her wit's end, but she couldn't convince her to abandon her boots.

"When will I see you again?"

"A lot sooner than you think. Call me if you need anything. Love you."

"Love you too!"

Suniya hung up the phone and burst into tears. She loved her mom so very much it hurt, She just didn't know how to make their relationship as mother and daughter work without interference from the demons of their past. Little did she know that her mother was across town weeping for the exact same reason.

CHAPTER 4

Tyreese was like a bored teenage boy aimlessly playing with his dick because he had nothing else to do when he heard Sade's Lexus pull up next door. Running to the window he watched as she pulled a bunch of shopping bags from her car and headed for her front door. Bolting to the door he quickly opened it and called to her.

"Hey Miss Sade! I see you've been shopping."

Struggling with the armload of bags she eyed him. "Hey Tyreese! What are you up to?"

"Not much… I'm trying to fuck something! What's up with you?"

A devious grin slowly spread across Sade's pretty face. She stared at the handsome, half dressed man that called to her from the porch next door. Her hormones quickly kicked into gear and her mind considered the possibility of some afternoon delight.

"Come on girl… Stop fronting like you don't want some of this hard dick." Tyreese said as he tugged on his erect dick through his black sweat pants.

"You know, you could at least offer me some help with my bags."

"Fuck that! You're crazy if you think I'm going in that man's house uninvited."

"What? I just invited you!"

"A man's house is his castle and I'm not going to disrespect Mason in his. So, come over here when you finish. I've been thinking about that fat ass of yours all day."

"You know what? You're as lazy as hell Tyreese! Many times as you've been up and through here with your funky ass! Whatever!" Sade vented before stomping into the house and slamming the door.

Tyreese grinned as he headed back into his house. He didn't bother to lock the door, because he knew his next door neighbor, Sade would be right over begging for a cup of dick cream. Sliding his unwashed ass onto the expensive contemporary chaise in the parlor he waited for her with his hard, monstrously thick dick in his hands.

His right hand was methodic as it stroked the length of his veiny manhood in an effort to get it ready for Sade's warm, accommodating mouth. His eyes rolled closed as he continued to slowly stroke himself from root to tip and back again. Licking his hand he added saliva to the mix to decrease drag and the burn of the friction on the loose skin as his hand slipped back and forward. His eyes tumbled around in his head as the sensation of his persistent hand quickly took him to a happy place.

Moments later Sade arrived. She had been there many times before and she knew the front door would be unlocked in preparation for her arrival. She didn't bother to ring the bell, she just came in and made herself at home. Falling at Tyreese feet she watched as he masturbated in the formal living room without a care in the world.

Her mouth watered as she watched his abnormally fat dick throb beneath the pressure of his strong hand. Sade's pussy instantly began to pump cream in anticipation of that anaconda slipping and sliding its chubby head in her swollen pussy. Aroused, she found herself rubbing her engorged clit as Tyreese continued to pleasure himself.

"Are you going to sit there all day watching me or are you going to take care of your dick?" Tyreese groaned.

Sade didn't answer. Her hand reappeared from between her thick thighs and replaced Tyreese's on his dick. It jerked as her soft hands stroked its stalk and swirled around its head. Noticing a bead of pre-cum at the tip, Sade gave the mushroom tip a hard lick and then an intense suck.

Tyreese's ass lifted from the silk, ivory colored chaise as she sucked it further into her throat. "Fuck yeah!" He groaned loudly as his hips gyrated against Sade's mouth. "Handle that damn dick, Sade! Handle it!"

Sade took it as a personal challenge and sucked Tyreese's diamond hard dick down her throat until she gaged. Gagging, choking and coughing she withdrew it and started all over again. Tyreese rewarded her efforts by grabbing a fist full of her weave to hold her head in place while he face fucked her. Gasping, spitting and slobbering she continued to swallow him whole.

Popping his dick from her mouth with a wet pop she searched Tyreese face. They made eye contact and she descended on his dick again while he watched. She knew how he loved to watch his dick disappear in her mouth one inch at a time. And she loved how it made his eyes roll back in head like brown, shiny marbles.

"Fuck! You taste so good!" She breathed around his dick.

"Don't get too comfortable down there. Me and you are about to go upstairs to my room and when we get there I'm going to split your ass open with this Kielbasa."

Sade grinned as her tongue curled around the purple bulbous head of Tyreese's dick. "I'm ready when you are."

CHAPTER 5

Suniya entered her family room hoping to be greeted by her live in boyfriend of two years with a welcome home hug and an affectionate kiss. Instead she was greeted by a mess. Half eaten Chinese food, beer bottles and empty containers cluttered her coffee table. The TV blared loudly and the air smelled of day old man must, ass crack and farts.

"This MF is about to work my last damn good nerve! Look at this damn mess!" She grumbled beneath her breath as she immediately began to clean up after a grown ass thirty year old trifling man. "Seriously, would it kill him to throw his garbage in the trash? This is ridiculous!"

It didn't take long to realize that she was talking to air. Where the hell is he?" Suniya questioned as she scanned the empty room. "Tyreese!" She called, but there was no answer.

It was a little past seven so she knew he wasn't in bed. Hell, half the time his lazy ass slept on the couch unless he wanted some ass. As she walked towards the powder room she heard a noise coming from the master bedroom. At first she thought she was hallucinating. So she stopped in her tracks and listened carefully. Then she heard it again.

Tip toeing quietly to the base of the stairs she strained her ear to hear. Her eyes widened as the sound grew louder and more intense. It was a distinct sound which she'd heard before.

"What the hell?" She thought as she processed the sound, unwilling to believe her ears. "Aw fucking hell naw!" She whined as she went to the bar and retrieved Tyreese's nine millimeter Glock pistol. "This bitch has just signed my damn arrest warrant."

Dropping the clip, she prayed it was loaded, it was. Popping the full magazine back in she disengaged the safety and slid the slide until a bullet loaded in the chamber. In retrospect she was glad Tyreese had insisted she learned how to handle the gun in case there was an intruder in the home. Little did he realize he was the intruder she'd one day have to expel from their home.

Suniya followed the sound of robust fucking to her master bedroom suite. Her nostrils flared with anger and the pungent smell of dick, pussy and ass. The closer she came to her bedroom the angrier she became. "Four bedrooms with two master suites in this fuckin house and this lazy fucker decides to fuck a bitch in mine! Unfucking real! I'm going to light his ass up like New Year's Eve if he's fucking on top of my new three hundred dollar duvet!" She growled beneath her breath as she reached the top of the stairs.

At this point Suniya was as mad as a bitch slapped with a million dollar alimony suit. She was so mad she started to see red blotches where objects should be. Suniya was drudging on a very dangerous path fueled by sheer rage and she knew it. Closing her eyes she sucked in a big breath as she tried to clear the fog of fury that had clouded her judgment. Ironically, the moment her eyelids closed she saw Sissy's face.

With tears in her eyes the vivid image of Sissy begged and pleaded for her to reconsider her course of action. "Boots, please don't do it! He's not worth it and you know it! Don't throw your life away for this trash. He doesn't deserve you. Put his freeloading, cheating ass out on the curb with the rest of the garbage. Boots, please put the gun down now! I need you in my life! Don't do it Boots! Please, don't hurt nobody."

"Okay momma." Suniya breathed as she wiped the lone tear that rolled along her cheek. She entered the bedroom locked and loaded and ready to fuck Tyreese's sorry ass up!

Now, even though she knew what was happening in the room before she entered, nothing could prepare her for the sight she would discover. Her eyes quickly scanned the rooms as she steadied her aim at the figures that moved on her king size bed. Adrenalin had flushed through her body and heightened her senses. Her eyes spotted one female who she quickly identified as her nosey, hot in the ass next door neighbor, Sade. Sade, whose nasty ass was about seven or eight months pregnant was being ass fucked on top of Suniya's expensive duvet. Cum stains and ass juice were splattered all over it.

Fury wrinkled her brow as Suniya identified the ass fucker. The second person was a male who Suniya instantly identified as Tyreese. Moving at warp speed he slammed his hard dick balls deep into Sade's ass without a damn condom. Suniya's head almost exploded with rage. It took everything she had to keep her from unloading her entire clip into his nasty, inconsiderate ass. He could have at least protected her by using a damn condom. She was officially furious.

Preoccupied neither of them noticed her presence when she entered the room. Suniya quickly rectified that with a pin point accurate shot to the bedside lamp. The glass lamp shattered into a hundred pieces, startling the two lovers.

"The next Mutha Fucka moves is getting some hot shit in the crack of their fuckin ass!" Suniya calmly announced with the gun pointed directly at them.

Frightened, Sade's big ass scrammed to get up to run but was pinned beneath Tyreese's bulky mass. Suniya fired a warning shot that pierced the wall just above the center of the white leather headboard.

"Bitch are you deaf and stupid? I just said do not move."

"Suniya, baby... I can explain. It's not what it looks like!"

"Tyreese, shut the fuck up and listen! I didn't ask for an explanation. In fact, I don't want to hear your voice ever again."

"Please, Suniya! Don't kill us! We just got caught up..."

"Seriously, Sade? Really? Didn't I just say I didn't want a damn explanation? So, do you really think I want to know why my boy friends dick is shoved up your pregnant ass?"

"Yessss... I mean no... Suniya don't kill me we can explain, right Tyreese?" Sade pleaded though Tyreese knew better than respond.

"Oh my God! Sade, please do us all a favor and shut the fuck up and listen! Okay? I'm serious... Make one more sound and see what happens!" Suniya screamed at the top of her lungs as she fired off another round which hit the headboard just above their heads. Sade's tear filled eyes bucked, but she didn't dare make a sound. "So, is everyone listening now?" Nobody said a word. They thought it was a trick question and dared to try the gun slinging sharp shooter. "Answer me damn it!"

"Yes!" They both screamed in unison.

"Good! Now, both of you get up, pack Tyreese's shit and get the fuck out of my house. If either of you ever speak of this I will unload my whole mag in your ass the next time I see you. It won't be pretty, you will not like it and you definitely will not survive. You have one minute so move! Now! Move!"

Tyreese climbed off of Sade, grabbed his clothes and shoes and quickly scrambled to put them on.

"Tick- tock, Tick – tock!" Suniya taunted as she watched the disoriented lovers dress at warp speed.

Tyree headed for the closet, but Suniya shot a warning shot in the wooden door frame that missed him by a baby's breath. She was well aware that he had a backup gun in a box in the top of his closet. "Don't fuck with me Tyreese!"

"Suniya, can I go home? My husband will be home in a few minutes. Please, I promise I won't tell anybody."

Suniya laughed at her. "Oh! I know you won't! What would you say, Sade? 'Officer, I was over at Suniya's house, fucking her sorry ass piece of man, in her bed, on her Egyptian silk duvet when she came home and threatened to bust a hot round in my nasty prego ass!' Is that how the conversation with the police would go? Huh, Sade? Yeah, I bet your husband would love to hear that! So, by all means, be stupid and open that can of worms." Sade who knew it was a rhetorical question didn't bother to aggravate Suniya by answering.

"Look Suniya, let her go. We'll sit down and discuss this like adults. This is between you and me, okay?" Tyreese pleaded. "Baby, I love you. We can work this out. One day, we'll laugh about this whole misunderstanding. Hell we may even tell our grandkids about it, someday."

"Sade, please leave. I'd hate for your hard working husband to come home and find out what a filthy piece of trash he married and impregnated." Suniya said as she rolled her eyes at Tyreese and refocused her attention to his partner in crime.

"Suniya, please don't tell Mason what happened. Please?"

"Sade, get your pregnant roach ass the fuck out of my house before your eggs hatch! Make sure you take Tyreese's crazy roach fucking ass with you!" Suniya sighed deeply and casually responded. Still holding Tyreese at gun point she announced, "Time's up Tyreese, you have to go!"

"What? You said I could pack my things! I'm not leaving without my shit!" He based.

"Get the fuck out of my house, right now!" Suniya screamed, punctuating her sentence with a shot at the floor between Tyreese feet.

Now Tyreese knew better than anyone just how accurate Suniya was with that weapon. Whatever Suniya aimed at, she hit. An ex-policeman, Tyreese trained her to be dead on accurate. If confronted, Suniya could take a man down with one shot. She was a natural marksman. So, he knew not to test her, yet he tried any way.

"Keep firing off rounds and you're soon run out of bullets. Do you even know how many bullets are left? I bet you didn't even check the clip when you grabbed it. Did you?" He taunted in an effort to confuse her.

"You know what? You're even stupider than Sade. Do I look like a fucking idiot? I'm a trained marksman."

"I ought to know, I'm the one that trained you." He retorted.

"Then you should know that the first thing I did was check my amo!" She snapped as she fired off two shots in succession that whizzed past his right and then his left ear. "Besides, I only need one to put your bitch ass down forever, so come on Tyreese and try me!"

"Alright! Alright! I'm leaving, but I'm coming back for my clothes and both of my guns. You can believe that shit Suniya Simmons!" He growled trying to intimidate her.

"Fuck you, Tyreese! You're not getting shit out of my damn house that I don't give you! Oh yeah, just so we are clear… If I find out your funky, broke dick ass has even ventured on my damn street, I will have my mother hire some thugs to make sure you never even breathe my name again. So bring your sorry, lazy, good for nothing, lack luster black ass back here for anything and they will never recover your body.

And if little Miss Nasty right there has anything to say, I'll make sure they bury her pregnant ass with you. Now get the fuck out of my house before I end you my damn self!" She snarled like a lion.

"Suniya, just so you know... I didn't see shit! I didn't hear shit! And I'm not going to say shit! Fuck you Tyreese, I'm out! Don't ever call me again." Sade declared as she threw up her hands in surrender and rushed towards the bedroom door.

"Sade, wait! What about the baby? You're caring my son, remember!" Tyreese yelled to her confused.

Sade stopped dead in her tracks and abruptly turned to confront him. "What baby? Naw, Boo-Boo you must be confused. This is my husband's baby. Okay? You were just dick and dick don't pay my damn bills! And Sade got a whole lot of needs and wants. Unfortunately for you, dick is just one of them. Our baby... Bitch please! Hell, your broke ass couldn't even buy my baby a bag of diapers, let alone a diaper bag. My baby is going to Medical School like his father. You can't even afford to send him to preschool, so fuck that! Like I said, don't call me no damn more!"

Suniya snickered beneath her breath and then composed herself. "Okay! Everybody out of my house before I forget I'm a Christian and break the commandment that says, 'Thou shalt not kill!' In other words, walk out now or get carried out later!"

Like an Olympic track star, Sade made a mad dash for the door and did not stop running until she made it safely inside of her house. Tyreese decided to stay and try to play on Suniya's emotions. He had no clue he had stomped her last fucking nerve weeks ago. Yes, the dick was good, but it wasn't worth the headache and the drama. Besides, she wasn't even getting any.

Tyreese was a womanizing freeloader who survived off the kindness and vulnerability of desperate and lonely women. Suniya knew that Sissy was right. She just refused to admit it to her. Tyreese had been on his way out of Suniya's life for months, he just didn't know it. She suspected he was cheating on her, but she just couldn't prove it until now. Essentially, she was just waiting for the right opportunity to put his trifling ass out.

"Suniya, don't do this. Baby give me some time to find a job and get myself together. If you put me out where am I supposed to go? You know, I don't have any money."

"Try hell, Tyreese. You've certainly earned a stay there!" She calmly responded as she motioned him towards the door with the barrel of her gun.

Tyreese eyed Suniya for a long breath and then decided to cut his losses and simply leave. Suniya never heard from him again.

CHAPTER 6

Mykal had been Atlanta for a little over a month and was no closer to finding Miss Right than he was when he first flew in from Miami. He was an extraordinarily handsome man, so pussy was served up on a silver platter everywhere he ventured in Atlanta. Unfortunately, that was not what he was looking for. He had been in the singles game long enough to know the difference between a hoe and a housewife. Mykal had his fill of pussy and he wasn't going to give into his carnal desires and miss his opportunity to live the fantasy of living happily ever after.

The problem was that Mykal was kind of a loner. He didn't really know anybody in Atlanta. In Miami, life was so different. Mykal knew everyone and they knew him. Here in Atlanta, he wasn't familiar with the night life and really wasn't interested in the bar or club scene. Mykal was looking for a woman who would not be found in that environment. He knew better than to search for a diamond in a pool of crystals, let alone a sea of glass.

So, he did not waste valuable time hanging out at various clubs. Mykal loved a good restaurant meal, but hated to dine alone. He usually just ordered from the delivery or take out menu. Chances of meeting anyone at a restaurant who was single was slim so, they were out at work.

Sure church was an option, but not a viable one for Mykal. Atlanta was the virtually the home of the Mega Churches and many of the clergy and upscale parishioners used Mykal's transport service. Subsequently, he'd been invited to and visited almost every Mega Church in Atlanta. What he found was that a lot of the women on the bar and club scenes were the same women circulating through the church, singing in the choir, preaching in the pulpit, praying for the sick and spearheading committees.

Mykal was a Christian, and he attended church regularly, but not every Sunday. He wasn't a hypocrite and realized that God was still working on him. Unfortunately, hypocrisy was running rampant in every church he visited. Everyone was trying desperately to be much more than they really were. Most of them had a hidden agenda and was ready and willing to do almost anything to promote and further whatever the hell they were trying to sale.

The women were just as materialistic, egotistic and conniving there as anywhere else, in his opinion. Some attended these churches with the specific intent to land a wealthy husband to take care of them and their children. If a man's car, clothes, shoes, watch, jewelry and financial portfolio wasn't up to their standard they would not even piss on him if he was on fire. Mykal had ducked, dodged and darted away from women like this his entire life. He hated hypocrites and opportunist and he refused to spend the rest of his life married to one. So, when Mykal attended church it was to get his praise on and nothing more.

The whole dating scene had become mind boggling to him. He couldn't believe that meeting a nice woman and dating had gotten so stupid. Hell, it was obvious why so many women were still single. Sure there may in fact be a shortage of good men, but the ones that were out there looking for a good woman were being brow beaten, duped, conned and interrogated to death. They were penalized simply because the last idiot the woman trusted to love her took a steaming shit on her heart and made her eat it before he left.

It was so sad to see so many damaged and confused women. Mykal thought it was just him, until he heard some guys at the company talking about it. He'd heard countless horror stories about guys getting caught up with a one night stand and having to pay child support for the rest of their life. In retrospect, he was glad that he'd always protected himself and made good choices.

On a much brighter note, Mykal's transportation business was thriving and prospering. At least he was on track in that aspect of his life. This was the real reason he moved to Atlanta in the first place. With the financial backing of Victoria he had purchased four helicopters to add to his existing fleet of ten limos and ten armored cars. Catering to the Atlanta elite, Mykal had all of his fleet equipped with bullet proof glass and driven by armed body guards. Each driver was military trained and licensed to correct a bitch should the need arise. The affluent Atlanta clientele loved it and subscribed to monthly and daily service.

Armor Bearer Elite Transportation quickly raised the standard and expectations of limousine and helicopter transportation service in the Atlanta area. The company was booked solid and flooded daily with new requests. Mykal couldn't keep up without expanding. So, he went into negotiation with his bank for funding to double his fleet within the next six months. They were happy to help and he was quickly approved for a substantial line of credit and an obscene bank loan.

Mykal's company was doing so well in fact, he was featured in the business section of a local magazine. There was no secret that Mykal owed a major portion of his success to Victoria. They had agree to give each other the space and opportunity to find new lovers. Victoria had graciously honored her commitment, but Mykal wanted to check on her. Besides, he owed every ounce of success he'd enjoyed to her, so he decided to contact her.

Mykal had not spoken to Victoria since he left for Atlanta. They had agreed that it was best. They both knew that Mykal would never stop seeing her if they maintained their friendship. More importantly, Victoria would never move on with her life.

Mykal pressed the speed dial for her number with mixed emotions. He honestly missed Victoria. Naturally his dick immediately changed positions the second her name popped in his head. It was automatic, he couldn't help it. Victoria Dickerson was hands down the sexiest woman he had ever encountered in thirty two years of life. Besides, Mykal was horny as hell. He had been handling his own business, so to speak, since he arrived in Atlanta and he was tired of it.

His body craved the familiar warmth of Victoria's mouth. She was his fantasy when he masturbated and like it or not his thoughts were drawn to her daily. Frankly, Mykal didn't like it. He hated needing anyone, especially a woman. So he put his phone back on his desk and tried to go back to work, but he couldn't. He needed to hear the sound of her voice.

"Oh this is ridiculous! Just call her. What's the big damn deal?" He vented to himself as he picked up his cell and called Victoria.

"Hello!" Victoria answered on the last ring without looking at the caller ID display.

"Hey Lady! You were on my mind so I thought I'd call you and make sure everything was alright. Did I catch you at a bad time?" She was silent. "Tori, do you know who this is? Hello? Hello? Tori, are you still there?" Mykal asked confused as he made sure his call had not been dropped.

Victoria wasn't expecting his call. His sultry voice ignited a current of electricity through her body that pulsed and burned like fire in her erotic core. "I'm here. Hey Rome." She quietly responded.

"Hey! Can you talk or did I catch you at a bad time?"

"Yeah! I mean, no! I can talk. You just caught me off guard. I thought we agreed to only contact each other unless it was an extreme emergency. Is everything okay?"

Now it was Mykal's turn to be silent. He was confused. He assumed she'd be ecstatic to hear from him, but for some reason she was distant, almost cold.

"Rome are you okay? If you need more money, just tell me. I'll have it wired to you immediately."

Naturally, this added hot sauce to his bruised ego. "I'm fine. I just called because I missed you. I didn't realize that it would be an issue if I bent the rules to say hi to my friend."

Victoria closed her eyes, drew a deep breath and blew it out slowly. "I'm not sure if it's against the rules or not. If my memory serves me correctly, you made the rules. I just went along with them."

"So what are you saying Tori? Are we done? That's it? No contact, no friendship, no nothing? Huh? Five years and you want to end it like this?"

"No! You don't get to put this on me, Mykal Roman. You left me! You wanted more than I had to give! You made the rules and I hated every one of them, but I loved you enough to respect your wishes. You told me our friendship as I knew it was over. It was you, not me! Remember?"

"Tori, I never said we couldn't be friends. I said we needed to put the brakes on the sex. The only way I knew how to do that was put some distance between our bodies and even that didn't work. Tori, I can't even touch my dick to take a piss without thinking about you!"

"I thought by now you would have found someone to take your mind off of me. Aren't you seeing anyone?" She asked baffled.

"No, not yet. I'm not trying to just hop on some pussy, because I want to fuck. I'm serious about finding a woman to settle down with. I just didn't realize that it'd be this damn hard. Women in Atlanta are on some new shit! They're even more money hungry and superficial than the women in Miami, believe it or not."

"Rome, women are women, no matter where they live. In the end we're all looking for the same thing."

"What's that?"

"A hard dick and a big thick wallet!" Victoria laughed. "Actually, we're looking for a king who is capable of providing a castle. And if he has a big old country dick… Well, that's just a bonus. "

"Well, I have one of those and I can buy ten castles. I'm just looking for a woman who can cook something other than Oodles of Noodles and a damn salad." Mykal chuckled. "Is that asking for too much? I mean if I'm off base then let me know."

"You can't cook a salad!"

"I know! Try to tell that to these can't boil water, gold grubbing tricks that are pursuing me! I love to get my dick sucked as much as the next guy, but a brutha wants a woman who can put a meal on the table every now and then. Honestly, I have no problem bringing home the bacon, but damn is it that hard to find a woman who knows how to cook it?" Victoria burst into laughter. "You're laughing but I'm serious. I don't even know why I'm preaching to the pulpit."

"Oh, hold up there Mr. Roman. Don't you dare lump me in with those losers. I know how to cook. Just because I don't have to cook does not mean I don't know how. I can throw down in the kitchen."

"What does your lettuce eating, skinny butt know about cooking?" Mykal laughed.

"What do you want to eat?"

"You know damn well what I want to eat!" Mykal chuckled. I don't know why you asked me that damn question. I'm so fucking horny, I'm about to fuck this stray cat that's been hanging around my office, just so I can say I had some Atlanta pussy!"

"Oh my God!" Victoria laughed. "Don't call me to post your bail when they lock your nasty ass up for unusual and unnatural cruelty to animals. We're going to have to do something before it comes to that."

Mykal's dick instant stiffened and went on pussy alert. "Yeah, I think you're right."

Victoria heard the inflection in his voice and knew what Mykal really wanted to eat. "So, what are you saying?" She tested the waters.

"I'm saying, get your fine ass on a plane, if you can sneak away from Tricky Dick."

"Tricky Dick and I are no longer married. We were officially divorced a few weeks ago."

"Wish I could say I was sorry, but I can't. Did you make out okay?"

"Yeah, I didn't do too badly, twenty mil plus an extra ten to shut the fuck up." She giggled.

"D-A-Y-U-M! I'm happy for you. Now get on a plane, hell buy one if you have to! I'll pick you up at the airport."

"This is counterproductive. You know that right?"

"I don't give a damn what it is!" Mykal assured her. "I want to see you. The only reason I'm not getting in Victory- 1 and heading to the airport is because I have an important meeting tomorrow morning at seven thirty."

"What's Victory- 1?" Victoria asked puzzled.

"A helicopter. Thanks to you I have four of them and six on order. So, I named them all after you, Victory- 1 through 10."

"Wow! I'm flattered! So, we're making money?"

"Tori, we're making so much money, the bank thinks I'm printing money! I'm completely booked for an entire year. I had to go to the bank to double the fleet, just to keep up with the demand. I called to let you know that I'd be able to repay you within the year."

"Rome, I am so happy for you. I knew you could do this. Don't worry about my money, just let it ride as an investment. I have more money than I could spend in a lifetime. You were right. Atlanta was a good move for you."

"The only thing that's wrong with Atlanta is you're not here. So, fly up for a week or two, so we can celebrate! Just say the word and I'll have my assistant book your flight."

Victoria nervously chuckled. "Let me think about it."

"Come on Tori. Why not?" Mykal whined as Victoria shut him down.

"You know why."

"Tori, please don't make me beg."

"Give me a couple hours to think it over. Okay?"

"Not really, but what choice do I have?"

Victoria was silent for an uncomfortable moment. "Okay, well I'll call you back with my decision."

"Alright, well I get off in an hour so call me back as soon as you decide what you want to do. I'll talk to you later." Mykal reluctantly agreed before hanging up.

CHAPTER 7

Victoria hung up and contemplated her decision with mixed emotions. She wanted to pass, but the persistent thump in her pussy wouldn't allow it. She hadn't been with anyone since Mykal left and she was just as horny as Mykal was. There was just one problem.

Before he left Miami, Mykal made it quite clear he wanted a life that included a wife and children. Victoria respected that. Although she had been in Atlanta since the day after Mykal's plane landed there she never once contacted him. He had no idea she was less than a thirty minute ride away.

Victoria's intent was not to follow him although it appeared as if that was exactly what she did. She didn't want to freak him out and appear as a crazy stalker, so she deliberately left him alone. He deserved to be happy and she was determined to leave him alone so he could find what he was looking for. Neither of them ever fathomed it would take this long to start dating again.

Atlanta was a new place and Victoria was afraid of hooking up with the wrong type of man. The world was filled with seedy creeps and Atlanta appeared to have more than its fair share. Victoria was alone and she refused to make herself a target by hanging out at clubs and bars alone.

Escorts were definitely out of the question. The harsh reality of the escort world was that most male escorts would go both ways if the price was right. The last thing Victoria wanted, or needed was a man on the down-low passing along something she couldn't get rid of or kill with a shot of penicillin.

Mykal Roman had been her safe spot. She knew he was healthy and meticulously safe. He was her one and only lover for the past five years. It was a no brainer. Besides, Victoria really missed her safe spot.

One hour later, Victoria found herself in one of Mykal's super stretch limos waiting outside the door of his office. She could have called and confessed that she was already in Atlanta, but this way was so much better. Besides, she knew that it'd be hard for Mykal to argue with a mouth full of delicious pussy.

Victoria had paid Clark, her driver a humongous tip to keep his mouth shut. The drivers all knew of Victoria although none of them had ever personally met her. Mykal established her role as his silent partner when he broke down the history and organization of the company. He spoke fondly of her and they all picked up on the fact that she was a little more to him than just a financial partner.

Clark had called Mykal's driver to assure that Mykal had not left the office. Being the owner of a transportation had its perks. Mykal rarely if ever drove to work. He hated the congested Atlanta traffic and didn't really know his way around the city that well. It made since for him to have his own personal car and driver to transport him safely wherever he needed to go.

All systems were a go and Mykal headed out front to meet his driver. Instead he found Clark waiting with a chromed out, custom built, black Cadillac Escalade super stretch. Needless to say he was a little confused and not at all amused.

"Right this way sir." Clark greeted him as he approached.

"What's going on? Where is Leonard and the Mercedes? And why are you here. I thought you were on an emergency run across town?"

Mykal had a ton of questions and Clark had no answers. So, he simply smiled. "I'll explain everything once you get in sir."

Mykal suspiciously eyed the driver. Mykal had handpicked Clark himself. He knew Clark was a no nonsense Marine who was in Special Forces. Mykal could trust Clark with his life. Normally he wouldn't hesitate to climb in the backseat of the vehicle, yet this time he did.

"Clark, I'm not in the mood for no bullshit! It's Friday and I want to get home as soon as possible. So, where the hell is my damn car?" He snapped.

Victoria had heard enough. Rolling down the window she called to him. "Oh for God sakes Rome... Just get in the damn car!"

Mykal's dick leaped in his pants at the sound of her sexy voice. He could not believe his eyes. A smile as bright as sunshine illuminated his face as his eyes fell on the beautiful blonde. "Victoria Dickerson. I have never been so happy to see you." Adjusting his hard dick in his tailored slacks, he gave Clark an apologetic nod and climbed in the back seat of the limo.

"Enjoy your ride sir." Clark discreetly smiled as he closed the limo door.

"Woman, how in hell did you get to Atlanta so quick?" Mykal attempted to ask, but Victoria threw herself in his arms and covered his mouth with a searing hot kiss. It had been months since she'd been in his arms and she refused to wait a single second longer.

Grabbing a fist full of her long, blonde highlights, Mykal kissed her with the resolve and intensity of a wounded soldier returning from a losing battle. Their tongues reconnected and danced a familiar dance as Victoria unzipped Mykal's pants and unleashed the beast that begged to be freed.

Her soft hand stroked him firmly as their eyes met for the first time in months. Words could not do what they felt, at that particular moment. justice so nether of them attempted to speak. Mykal planted a line of tender kisses along Victoria's jawline that led to her luscious lips. Once there he smothered her mouth with his.

Time seemed to stand still as the lovers kissed as if the world would end if they dared stop. They never even realized that Clark had pulled off. Mykal had no clue where they were headed and frankly he didn't give a damn. Where ever Victoria was headed was exactly where he wanted to be.

Mykal's hand slid between her thighs and revealed his suspicions. Victoria had a secret, she was not wearing any panties. A deep primal groan escaped her throat as two of his long, thick fingers slipped into her tight pussy and stroked her pleasure palace.

Victoria's body gyrated slowly on his hand in search of an orgasm that had been building in her womanhood since the moment she heard his voice on the phone earlier that day. Mykal wasn't the only one who had been deprived of the warmth of a human's touch. Victoria was equally sex starved and in desperate need of some dick.

Breaking their lip lock she slipped her slinky, form fitting dress off revealing her magnificent nude frame. Mykal's eyes sparkled at the sight of her. Pulling her close he sucked on her breasts as he resumed finger fucking her. It felt wonderful, but Victoria had something else in mind.

Pushing Mykal back onto the large bench seat she maneuvered herself into the sixty nine position. It was clear they both were starving so she figured they might as well have a snack. She had no complaints from Mykal, he attacked her pussy as if he was the reigning champion in a pussy eating contest.

His tongue lick ravenously at the pool of juice which had collected between the lips of her pussy. Once it was all gone he licked within its wall in search of more. His tongue was wet and warm as it stroked her inner walls driving her within a split second from insanity.

Growling something which Mykal could not understand she squeezed his balls and attempted to swallow his shaft whole. Victoria was driven like a maniac and refused to stop until Mykal's big dick choked her. Coughing, sputtering and slobbering, she feverishly jerked the loose flesh of his dick before swallowing it again.

Mykal's eyes rolled around in his head like two corkscrew marbles. As she hollowed her cheeks and sucked his hard dick into her mouth repeatedly. The suction capacity of Victoria's mouth was as deadly as any weapon of mass destruction. Mykal's dick had longed for a reunion with Victoria's mouth. Hell, it even preferred it to her hot pussy.

His climax swell quick causing his body to jerk and twitch with the intensity of his rapidly approaching core melt down. Grabbing the back of her head he fucked her mouth hard as he devoured her clit. Sucking, nibbling and gnawing on it like a puppy's milk bone he soon coached her to the edge of a nuclear explosion as well.

Sounds of whimpering, sucking, groans and growls blended seamlessly with the smooth contemporary R&B that permeated the sexually charged atmosphere.

Mykal felt his body lock and seize mid stroke as he gyrated hard against Victoria's eager mouth. He knew he was done, so he didn't try to fight it, he simply let go. Screaming like a frightened girl running through the woods being chased by the Boogie Man, Mykal released hard into the back of Victoria's throat. His thick, hot semen joked her as it sprayed against her gag receptors.

Gagging uncontrollably she tried to swallow as much of it as she could. Squirt after squirt coated her throat. She thought he would never stop coming and so did Mykal. He had never come so hard in his entire life. His spirits seemed to float from his body and hover above the naked couple. For a split second he was convinced he was knocking at the pearly gates.

Just when he thought he couldn't take it one second more Victoria slurped the last of his hot juices down her throat. Appreciative, he grabbed Victoria by her ass pulling her swollen pussy closer to his mouth. Without hesitation he devoured her pussy like it was homemade sweet potato pie on Thanksgiving Day. When he was finished Victoria was floating on a cloud of pleasure in route to Pleasure Island.

Victoria's orgasm was so intense her body went limp and she collapsed without warning or a single sound. Sensing she was done and possibly semi-comatose Mykal gathered her in his arms and held her tight until she slowly revived. Kissing her delicate shoulders softly he asked, "Where are we headed?"

Victoria hugged him tighter and quietly breathed. "My place."

CHAPTER 8

Two months had passed since Suniya caught her live in boyfriend, Tyreese butt plugging her pregnant neighbor in their damn bed. There wasn't enough eyewash and Visine in the world to get that nasty image out of her head. She instantly succumbed to her fiery anger every time she thought of it. Her imported Egyptian silk duvet was ruined and had to be trashed along with the rest of her bedding. Her headboard was ruined from the bullet she fired into it but she kept it to remind her just how bad ass she was.

Fortunately, Tyreese had the decency and good common sense to never contact her again. So, she trashed the bulk of his junk and gave his nice things to Good Will. Naturally she kept the two handguns, just in case she ran across another bitch that desperately needed to be corrected. The one and only downside to the whole fiasco was Suniya had to see that pregnant cockroach, Sade every damn day.

What really pissed her off the most was that after all the dust had finally settled Sade was the only one who came out of it virtually unscathed and squeaky clean. Sure, Sade was still a little shell shy and avoided direct contact with Suniya like the flesh eating Eboli virus, but she got off too easy. Mason, her husband never had a clue what her trifling ass was doing while he was at work. So, her life went on as if the incident never happened.

Tyreese on the other hand lost almost everything. He lost his home, his clothes, his meal ticket, his dignity and his cash cow, Suniya. Suniya had been taking care of his silly ass since the day they met. Tyreese was on administrative leave from the Police department pending dismissal when they met. Apparently a large amount of narcotics and weapons disappeared from the evidence room under his watch. Tyreese swore to Suniya that it was all a big misunderstanding and he would be reinstated in a matter days. Naturally, totally mesmerized and seduced by his Atlanta swag, charisma and Macho bullshit, Suniya believed him.

She was captivated by the tall, dark handsome Atlanta policeman. Tyreese was exceptionally tempting to the eyes. Standing at six feet two inches tall and built like a male fitness model he was an impressive specimen of manhood. Dark coco skin, brilliant white teeth and a dimpled smile just sealed the deal. Suniya had to have him. They met on a Saturday and Tyreese was practically living with her by the following Wednesday.

Initially, Suniya didn't mind footing the bill for their dates and loaning Tyreese money. Hell, she even paid most of his many bills. Although he never been married, Tyreese had three children by three baby mamas and Suniya helped with his court ordered, child support payments as well. The way she saw the situation, it was worth it.

Tyreese was an animal in bed. He could have easily been classified as a ferocious beast with an insatiable appetite for wet pussy. Suniya couldn't keep him off of her and she didn't want to. Sex with him was like a Six Flag's adventure ride and Suniya had a season tickets and a back stage pass. Then one day everything changed.

Well, everything except Tyreese address. Days turned into months and eventually his hearing came. Tyreese lost his job and due to the nature of the dismissal his law enforcement career was officially over. Hell, Tyreese couldn't even get a flashlight security job at McDonalds. Too proud, too stubborn and too arrogant to do anything except soak in self-pity, he took up residence on Suniya's couch. In fact the only time he left it was to eat, shit or fuck.

Suniya instantly recognized it for what it was, extreme depression. She felt sorry for him and did everything within her means to lift his spirits and keep him happy. Smothering him with motherly love Suniya did everything for Tyreese except cut his food. Soon, he became so slothful he wouldn't even consider looking for a job. In fact, Tyreese had become so lazy he wouldn't even take a blow job. In retrospect, Suniya realized that her mothering of Tyreese essentially crippled and killed their relationship.

Two years later, Tyreese barely spoke to her, let alone fucked her. It appeared to Suniya that he made love to her more out of obligation than desire and she was right. Tyreese resented her and hated the fact that she was more man than he'd ever been in his entire adult life. Crippled by his own insecurities and self-loathing he could not see that she was only trying to help.

He also could not see that in order to get back on his feet and back into the world he had to assist in his own rescue.

Fortunately, getting caught with Sade was Tyreese's first step in regaining his independence. After he was violently ripped from Suniya's motherly tit, Tyreese found a job, moved into his own apartment and went back to school. He had no other choice. If he didn't continue to make his child support payments on time he'd end up in jail. An ex-cop in jail was a death sentence and Tyreese knew it, so he took the first job he could find and took his ass back to work were he belonged.

It's funny how staring down the barrel of a loaded 9mm handgun can change your whole existence. Sade even changed after the event. Scared straight, she became the model wife. Her husband was a kind, hard- working man who cherished her and he deserved nothing less than the best. Mason was the only reason Suniya didn't expose Sade as the dirty, nasty, gold digging cheat she was. He deserved better and Sade decided that after what she went through dealing with Tyreese's worthless ass, it was time for her to do better.

It appeared on the surface that everyone got their act together, so Suniya was determined to do the same. She vowed to never take care of another man who did not pass through her womb as her child. Suniya also vowed never to sleep with a man without a ninety day grace period. Ninety days was ample time for her to figure out if a man was psycho, homeless, unemployed, married, gay, abuse, lazy, a liar or plain crazy.

So, Suniya instantly instituted the no physical contact for ninety days dating clause and added it to the top of her, "Don't fuck with me unless you are correct list." Now, this seemingly endless list of do's and don'ts for would be suitors was really just a formality since she wasn't actively dating. In fact, Suniya was too busy with her new business to even think about dating. She had endured too many trifling men to consider wasting her precious time with another at this point in her life.

Her boutique was the most important thing in her life and quickly became her major focus. It required all of her time and her effort. Managing her new men's store was physically and emotionally draining and left Suniya with absolutely no time to chase dick, even if she wanted to. So, dating was put on the back burner and the vibrator was moved from the closet to the bedside table.

Suniya was on a mission to make her unique male boutique a huge success. She was young and beautiful so she had plenty of time to search for Mr. Right. She soon realized that if he really was Mr. Right, he'd be searching for her. If so, he'd find her at the Gentlemen's Essentials Boutique.

CHAPTER 9

Fall fell upon Atlanta quickly as time moved on. Mykal looked around his office and discovered his chauffeurs were in desperate need of coats. Each driver was required to be appropriately dressed in a black tailor custom suit, crisp white shirt and black tie. Their uniform was identical down to their black silk socks.

Unfortunately, Mykal had not considered the change in weather and the need for overcoats. The temp dropped overnight in Atlanta one early fall day and lingered on the colder side of fall. Most of the guys just grinned and bared it, but the female drivers, who wore below the knee pencil skirts instead of slacks were quite vocal.

"Mr. Roman, can we speak with you for a second?" Kayla asked accompanied by two other female drivers, Jessica and Cherie.

"Sure, come in ladies and have a seat." Mykal smiled as he put the paperwork he was working on aside and welcomed them into his office.

"Thank you sir, but we'll stand. This will only take a second." Jessica responded and they all nodded in agreement.

"Okay…What can I do for you?" Mykal eyed them, a little puzzled by their visit.

Kayla waited for one of the other women to start, but no one spoke up, so she started the dialogue. "Mr. Roman, we know you're probably aware that the weather has changed since we first opened in early spring."

"Yes! Atlanta weather is a little brisker than what I'm accustomed to. Miami was never this cool this time of year. I'm considering turning on the heat in my condo if it doesn't warm up soon." Mykal chuckled.

"See, that's the thing sir… Atlanta gets pretty cool at night. It's unlikely that the temperature will rise much as the days go on. In fact, it probably will get colder if anything."

"I'm not sure I understand were this conversation is headed." Mykal responded, now completely lost. It was obvious that the three women wanted something, but he couldn't figure out exactly what. "Exactly, what are we talking about, because I'm sadly lost as to why we're discussing the weather?"

"Sir, we were just wondering what we should do as far as outer attire when we are on duty." Cherie replied.

"We don't want to be cited for being out of uniform, but we're freezing out there in these skirts." Jessica chimed in.

"It's a lot easier for the men to keep warm, but we need coats." Kayla declared. "We don't mind finding matching coats for the three of us to wear... We'll even pay for them... We just need your permission to wear them while on duty."

"I am so sorry. I never even considered the fact that you needed coats. Don't worry about a thing, find the coats and I'll pay for them of course. Why didn't someone tell me there was a problem?"

"We just did." Cherie giggled.

"We love our jobs, so we try not complain, but our little legs are freezing out there." Jessica added.

"The guys carry a lot more bulk and most of them trained in adverse weather, so they'd never complain." Kayla chimed in. "We just wanted to bring it to your attention before winter fell."

"I understand and please forgive my oversight. By all means, get whatever you need and charge it to the company card. As matter of fact, get a pair of boots as well." Smiles instantly transformed the three women's concerned faces as Mykal spoke.

"What about the guys?" Jessica asked.

"I guess I can look online and try to find a men's clothier with decent overcoats." Mykal replied. "Don't worry I'll take care of them. You ladies pick out the boots and coats you like and I'll shop for the men."

"The reason I asked is because my husband just purchased a very nice cashmere blend coat at this place not far from here. His coat was very reasonable and is a very good quality, maybe they can help you there." Jessica responded as she passed Mykal a business card.

Mykal smiled as he took the card. "Thanks, you've just made my task so much easier. I'll call them today... On second thought, I could use an overcoat as well, so I'll drop by there this afternoon."

~*~*~

Mykal made a few phone calls as his driver transported him to the boutique. His day was hectic, but he needed a coat as bad as the rest of his staff. He only hoped they had what he was looking for.

Leonard maneuvered the Mercedes in front of the quaint boutique just as Mykal got on the phone with Victoria.

"Hey, how's your day going, or should I even ask?"

"Don't ask... It's crazy as usual. I had to make a quick run away from the office. When I get back, I have three meetings back to back." He sighed. "So, please tell me that we're still on for tonight. I need to work out some of this frustration."

"You're the last person on this planet that should be sexually frustrated. My neck is still stiff from the last time you worked out your frustrations on me." Victoria laughed.

"Yeah, but it had been a while. Besides, I never said I was sexually frustrated. How could I be sexually frustrated when I have a beautiful creature at you crawling in and out of my bed regularly? So, what time are you coming through to bless me with some of that honey love?" His sexy baritone voice flirted.

"I'm afraid I have a fund raiser benefit that I have to attend tonight. I probably won't be done there before midnight. Sorry, you and Jergens are on your own tonight."

"What? Stop playing Tori. I've been looking forward to this date all week. I don't care what time you finish, have the driver drop you off at my place. I need to see you."

"No... What you need to do is stop relying on me to satisfy that itch in your pants and get back to finding a permanent solution to your problem."

"Yeah, I know but…"

"Look, ever since we started hooking up again, you've put this thing on the back burner. We both know how this is going to end, badly. I don't want to get all cozy with you Rome, only to be dumped on my ass again. We want different things out of a relationship. I can only give you fifty percent of what you're looking for."

"Why do you have to make this so hard? When we're together it is what it is. I may never find what I'm looking for. Let's just roll with it until I do. Okay?"

"Rome… Why can't you see that I'm the one that will get hurt if I allow myself to get caught up on you with no backup plan?"

"Tori, we'll always be friends." Mykal sighed in frustration. "I'd no more hurt you than I'd hurt myself."

"Maybe, but I'd still end up hurt."

"So, are you stopping by tonight or what?"

Victoria hesitated for a long breath. "I'll be there when I'm done."

Mykal hung up the phone and considered the conversation he just had with Victoria. Naturally, he could read between the lines and detect that Victoria's feelings were getting a little too involved and she didn't want to get hurt. Unfortunately, he wasn't prepared to release her until he found her equal. Yes, it was selfish, but the truth of the matter was that he had feelings for her as well.

Feelings or not, Mykal knew that a life without children was just not an option for him. It may be okay for Victoria, but it wasn't for him. He knew Victoria was right. Mykal had stopped looking for a woman the moment he found out that Victoria had moved to Atlanta. A part of him didn't feel the need to continue the search.

Victoria was all the woman he needed. They were perfect together. Sadly, she was adamant about not having children and refused to even discuss the issue. Mykal didn't know why, but he knew it had something to do with her past. If only he could convince her to reconsider.

"We're here Mr. Roman." Leonard announced, interrupting his train of thought.

Mykal looked out the window just as a beautiful woman opened the door to enter the boutique. "Dayum!" He breathed as he caught a quick glimpse of the juiciest onion booty he had ever encountered. Leonard coughed to keep from laughing out loud at Mykal's response. "Leonard did you see that?"

"Yes sir! I did!" The chauffer responded in his most professional voice. "Are we ready to go in sir?"

"Yeah! I'm ready." Mykal recovered as he continued to stare at the entrance of Gentlemen's Essentials.

CHAPTER 10

Mykal went to Gentlemen's Essentials with one and only one thing in mind. He was there to purchase overcoats for his staff and possibly himself. However, when he entered the boutique his eyes instantly scanned the facility for the woman whose round ass made his dick leap to attention.

It had been a very long time since a woman, other than Victoria, had elicited that type of response from Mykal. He was constantly in the presence of extraordinarily gorgeous women, yet his dick did not budge. It was trained to behave. Then, this woman crosses his sight for a millisecond and he can't keep his dick from getting hard just thinking about her.

After a quick initial scan she was nowhere to be found. It was as if she just disappeared into thin air. Mykal entered the store no more than five minutes after her, so she couldn't have gotten that far. It puzzled him where she could have vanished to that fast. Then he heard a soft sexy voice over his shoulders that caused the hairs on his balls to stand up.

"Hi, I'm Suniya. Can I help you find something today?"

"Aw fuck! This is not going to end well." He thought to himself as he discreetly readjusted his menacing dick in his pants. Buttoning his suit jacket he attempted to hide it before facing her.

Mykal's eyes fell on the stunning Suniya Simmons for the very first time and the rhythm of his heart instantly increased. She smiled at him and as if by magic a sexy smile spread across his face like sunshine in early spring.

"Hi, Suniya. I'm Mykal." His sultry voice informed her.

"Nice to meet you, Mykal. Welcome to Gentlemen's Essentials. You look a little disoriented. Is this your first time?"

Mykal nervously chuckled. "Yes! Although I must admit that's probably not why I look perplexed, but let's go with it."

"Okay." Suniya giggled.

Something about this man threw her off her game. Sure he was tall, dark and so very handsome, but that wasn't it. Surprisingly, he was well dressed, groomed and polished with an evolved fashion sense. Suniya ran a men's clothing store, and soon discovered that very few of the men who ventured in her boutique really knew exactly how to dress.

This man was different. Mykal was fashionably dress from his head down to his feet and all parts in between. Everything about him screamed, "I have money!" Yet, he had an easiness to him that calmly spoke, "So what? I don't care... That's not important."

Suniya stepped back a step from him as his sexy, broad, perfect smile made her spirit dance. It frightened her and so did he. It had been almost three months since she kicked Tyreese out of her house. Since then the only men that had been in her bed room was Ben and Jerry and occasionally Jack Daniels. So, her instant attraction to Mykal was alarming to say the least.

A part of her wanted to turn him over to one of the sale associates, but that would have been a waste of time. The two associates working with her were both women and they were staring Ga-ga Goo- goo eyes at Mykal from the front desk. Essentially they would be about as useful as tits on a bull, so she had to tough it out. Then another part of her just wanted to melt all over that Italian, hand tailored suit like warm butter on hot popcorn.

Normally, she'd put her infatuation for a handsome customer to the side and do her job, but not this time. Suniya's pussy was thumping so loud she was afraid that Mykal might hear it. She wanted to run to the bathroom and plug the endless flow of cream it was pumping with a wad of tissue, but her legs wouldn't move. Luckily she had not lost her ability to speak so she used that to her advantage. It would sustain her until his haunting glare released the rest of her body from its spell.

"So what can I do for you this afternoon?"

Mykal chuckled as he considered what he really wanted Suniya to do for him. He couldn't believe he was being so damn crass and naughty. He wasn't horny. Victoria took care of that the night before. He didn't know what was going on. So, he decided to tackle it head on.

"What's so amusing?" Suniya smiled.

"Honestly… You are. Look, Suniya, I normally do not act this way. I'm kind of out of sort for some reason. So, I'm just going to go ahead and address the pink elephant in the room."

Suniya burst into laughter. "Oh my God! Did you just imply that I was fat? I know I put on a pound or two, but there's really no need for name calling."

Mykal's face blushed as he looked down and noticed that Suniya had on a pink blouse. Embarrassed, he immediately began to back pedal. "I am so sorry! That was not what I meant! You have to believe me!"

Suniya continued to laugh. It felt good to know that she had an effect on him as well. "It's okay, I was just teasing you. Do go right ahead and address the pink elephant in the room that is not named Suniya." She teased.

Mykal bit his lip and smiled at the beautiful young woman. Her sense of humor was refreshing. Her laughter was contagious and her bright smile set his heart on fire. He had to get to know her.

"Okay... Is there someone else here that could help me, because I can see we're not going to get a thing accomplished today." He chuckled.

Suniya looked over where her two associates were standing, ease dropping. Their mouths were unhinged as they hung on every word that came out of Mykal's mouth. Returning her attention back to Mykal she declared, "Nope! Afraid not. Besides, I have to hear this."

"Okay, then I'm going to just put myself out there. Suniya, you are one of the most beautiful women I've ever met. If I appear disoriented it is because you beauty has arrested me. I say this with the utmost respect. If you're single would you consider having lunch with me one day? Please?"

Suniya's heart leaped at the invitation, yet she was reserved. This was not her first time around the Pretty Boy tree. Suniya had given up on men for all practical purposes. Naturally, she was hit on and asked out daily. Never once did she even consider saying yes until this very moment.

Her eyes slowly scanned the handsome stranger who wandered into her store and instantly set her panties on fire. She realized she could do a hell of a lot worse, but she was convinced she was ready for another dose of man drama.

She smiled politely. "Let me think about it while we find what you need."

Mykal sighed deeply. Her answer wasn't a hard no, but it also wasn't a yes. He understood that Suniya was at work, and apparently she was a professional. He smiled and gave her a nod to indicate that he understood perfectly. "Sure! That would be great."

"Good! What can I help you find today?"

"I'm looking for a full length overcoat, preferably one with a cashmere blend."

"What color? We have several very elegant styles that I can show you."

"Um, I need a navy blue and I need to see a black one in a different style."

"So, you need two coats?" Suniya asked confused.

"Actually, I'm going to need exactly twelve black and one navy coat."

Suniya was at a loss for words. "I don't understand."

"I own a transportation business and I need twelve coats for my drivers and a navy blue coat for myself. I should have explained it better, but I wanted to take a look at the coats first." He chuckled.

"Oh, okay. Well, right this way, I'll show you the selection that I have in stock and we can order whatever sizes you need."

"How long does that usually take?" Mykal asked as he followed the rhythm of Suniya's romp as it led him to the other side of the store.

"Just a couple of days. My distributors are pretty good at filling my orders promptly." Suniya responded as she felt the sting of Mykal's eyes on her round ass. Oddly enough she liked it, so she pretended not to notice. "Here we are. I have three styles in each color to choose from."

Mykal carefully considered each style coat as Suniya looked on. He could feel her eyes probing him especially when the fell on his crotch area. Like her he liked it so he pretended not to notice.

"These are very nice, it's a tough decision. Which design do you prefer more?"

"I guess it depends on the purpose. Are your drivers truck drivers or limo drivers or what?

"They're limo drivers."

"Then I'd go with this coat. It's an eighty- twenty cashmere and wool blend. It's very stately, durable and warm. Your drivers will love it and your clients will be very impressed."

"Yes, that's the one my mind had settled upon as well. Can you have twelve of them delivered by Monday?"

"Sure, it's Wednesday, so I don't see why not. I'll put the order in now if you like. What about the navy coat?"

"Actually, I'd like to be fitted for that one today, if that's possible."

"Certainly, I can take you to the fitting area and measure you right now."

"Great, I'm completely at your disposal."

Suniya led Mykal to an area with mirrors on every side. "Please take off your coat and let me just get your measurements. We like to keep them on file, for future reference, if that's okay?"

"Sure, I'll definitely be back for future purchases." He smiled as he slowly removed his suit jacket, revealing a tight, tone body that made Suniya's pussy swallow hard.

"Ah fuck!" She breathed to herself. Well, at least she thought she breathed to herself, although Mykal heard her.

"Is everything okay?"

"Yeah! I broke the lead on my pencil. Excuse me, I'll be back in one second, I have to get another one." Suniya didn't wait for a response from Mykal. Shaken, she bolted to a back room and struggled to compose herself.

Suniya had never met a man who could send her body into total chaos with one damn glance. Mykal's tall, muscular body rivaled that of any action figure imaginable. It had been a very a while since felt the warmth of a man between her thighs. Could this be the man she's been waiting for?

Suniya drew three deep cleansing breaths and put on her professional face. Clutching the clipboard that held her measurement form she returned to the measurement area to find Mykal sitting in an armchair with his legs crossed waiting for her.

"Sorry about that. I'm ready whenever you are."

A devious grin tugged at the corner of his mouth as he saw how flushed she was. Not one to gloat, he ignored it and stood in the center of the mirrored room with his arms raised high. "I'm all yours." He smiled.

Suniya knew he was toying with her. "You need to stop playing. This will go a whole lot quicker if you'd simply stop flirting and let me do my job."

Mykal chuckled, "Who me? What did I do?"

Suniya looked at him in the mirror as she continued to move around his body taking measurements. "Nothing, not a thing."

"I tried to address the elephant in the room. We'd be past this if you simply said yes."

"Perhaps I don't want to say yes."

"Then you need to report that memo to your body, because it's sending a totally different message." Mykal chuckled.

"This isn't funny. I'm working. Besides, I don't date my customers. It's bad for business."

"Then perhaps you should look for another job, because I'm not going to stop pursuing you until you go out with me."

"Don't you have somebody else you can badger? I'm really trying to take a break from drama, aka men."

"Oh yeah, how's that working out for you?" Mykal chuckled.

"Actually it was working just fine, until now." Suniya snickered as she measured Mykal's inseam.

Her warm hand brushed likely against his manhood and it instantly responded by changing position. Now, it was Mykal's turn to become flushed and embarrassed. Suniya pretended not to notice.

"Sorry about that." He apologized. "It wasn't intentional."

"Don't worry about it. It happens all the time." She nonchalantly responded as she completed her measurements. Wait right her and I'll bring your coat back for you to try on."

"Do you know which one I like?"

"I certainly do." She assured him with a bright smile. "Give me a second."

Dani one of her associates met her at the coat section. "So how big is it?"

"How big is what?" Suniya asked, pretending not to know what Dani was talking about.

"Seriously? Is this the game you want to play Suniya?"

"I have absolutely no idea what on earth you are talking about. How big was what?"

"What do you think?" Dani giggled. "Stop playing professional and dish the dirt. I have a bet with Jaye. All I need to know is small, medium, large or redunkulous."

"Now, that's a redonkulous thing to ask. I didn't measure his nature that would just be truly redonkulous."

Dani's hand flew over her mouth. "You lucky bitch! I can't stand you!"

Suniya pulled the coat down she was searching for, stuck her tongue out Dani and spun on her heels to walk away.

"I bet he's gay!" She called to her.

"I bet he's not!" Suniya called back as she headed across the store to the measurement room.

Mykal's coat fit perfectly, so he followed Suniya to the register to pay for it. "I need to set up appointments for my guys to be fitted. Should I call you?"

"Sure. I'll be here all day tomorrow."

"Great! We'll be back in the morning, so we can get this order in as soon as possible."

"So, you're coming with them?" Suniya asked confused.

"Somebody has to pay for it. Besides, it will give me another chance to see you in a different light. Who knows what you look like first thing in the morning?" He grinned.

"Certainly, not you." Suniya snickered.

"So are you single? I mean, I'm single, what about you?"

"Yes, the last time I checked."

"When was that?" he smiled.

"On second thought, maybe I'm not single. Does Ben and Jerry count?" Suniya joked.

"No! And you are definitely, single. So what about lunch?"

Suniya looked at the extraordinarily handsome man. Mykal, I don't really have time for games."

"Good, because neither do I. If you're not attracted to me than just say so and I won't bother you."

"What if I am?"

"Then just say yes to a lunch date. It's just lunch, Suniya. I promise, I'm a gentleman. What do you say?"

Suniya considered the offer and the man before her. She knew she'd kick herself if she didn't at least take the opportunity to find out more about him. "Okay! Let me put this order in and we can go to the deli around the corner."

"Great!"

"That would be great. Do you accept American Express?"

"Naturally." Suniya smiled. "Follow me."

"It'd be my pleasure."

CHAPTER 11

Mykal was ecstatic that Suniya agreed to have lunch with him. It was obvious some Bozo had clowned her and now she was guarded. He could only hope that she wasn't too damaged to let him in.

There was something about her that resonated with his spirit. Sure, there was the physical attraction. Hell, his dick almost bust his zipper when her melodious voice spoke to his name for the very first time. Still there was so much that transcended any physical attraction he ever felt for a woman.

Mykal didn't really believe in the concept of soul mates or love at first sight. Yet, he found himself coco flavored bananas for this woman who he never knew existed until an hour ago. Cruising his menu he stole a glance at her and prayed, "God please don't let this woman be obnoxious or pick her nose at the table or some other craziness."

Closing his menus and placing it on table beside him, he folded his hands together. He smiled as watched the beautiful Suniya as she contemplated her selection from the deli menu.

She seemed so perfect, so well put together, so exceptional, he knew something must be really wrong with her.

"What's wrong?" She asked still staring at the menu in her hand as if would magically change or tell her what to order.

"Nothing. For once everything seems perfect. I guess that's what scares me."

"Something must be wrong, because you keep staring at me as if I a dick were my nose should be." She casually responded as she flipped the menu over to look at the backside.

Mykal laughed. "Trust me, if you had a dick growing above your mouth, we wouldn't be sitting here and I definitely would not be staring."

"Why? You don't dick?"

Mykal chuckled, "Oh I love dick."

Suniya peered over here menu with an inquisitive eyebrow raised. "Oh really?"

"Yes! I love dick, my own that is. And I don't care to see another, especially on a face as beautiful as yours." He finished.

"So, is it safe to assume that you are not homosexual, bisexual, or curious? Sorry, but I have to ask for my own protection."

"No problem. I am one hundred percent heterosexual. I'm not curious about a damn thing. What about you."

"Nope, straight as a stripper pole." She nonchalantly answered, still hiding behind the menu.

"Speaking of stripper poles. Do have a favorite or have you had one attached to your ass in the last five years. Sorry, but I have to ask for my own protection."

Suniya smiled and placed her menu on the table and folded her hands just like Mykal's. "No. Any communicable diseases? You know... HIV, AIDS, Herpes, Chlamydia, Hepatitis, HPV or an itchy rash that just won't go away?"

"Never. I'm as a specimen of health. I haven't had much more than a cold in years. I get a physical, with blood work every single year and I'm extremely careful. You know what they say, safety first." He stared in to her eyes. "What about you?"

"Nothing, not even the occasional sniffles." She stared back with batting an eyelash. "Drugs?"

"No."

Gambling problems?"

"No."

"Spousal abuse?"

"Hell no!"

"So, you had a spouse?"

"No."

"Live in?"

"No."

"Side chick?"

"A friend, with benefits… Excellent benefits."

Suniya scanned Mykal from head to toe with her Bullshit Detector and surprisingly he came up clean. He was confident and borderline arrogant but she suspected he was telling the truth. Unfortunately the inquisition was not over.

"Commitment issues, I see." She smirk. "The worst flaw of them all. It ranks right up there with AIDS and herpes."

"Actually, you need your vision checked, because I don't have commitment issues. Not to say I don't have an issue, that's just not it. Never felt the desire to commit, until recently."

Suniya looked puzzled. "So what changed?"

"I woke up one morning in a bachelor apartment alone, and realized that I was getting to old to run the streets like I was a kid. After that I took a long look at how I chose to live my life to that point and decided to make some changes."

"So how old are you, if you don't mind me asking?"

"I'm thirty two. How old are you?" Mykal replied as he took a sip of his water.

"Who me, I just turned seventeen last month." She teased.

Mykal eyes bucked as he instantly choked on his water. Spitting water across the room narrowly missing Suniya, he struggled to catch his breath. "Are you serious?"

Suniya laughed. "No, I just wanted to mess up all that cool, calm and collective exterior you're projecting from over there. I'm actually, fifteen."

"Woman, don't play like that. A statutory charge is nothing to play around with."

"Trust me, it'll be a long, long time before you even come close to doing anything to me that could remotely be misconstrued as sexual." Suniya snickered.

"What are you talking about?" Mykal stared at her suspiciously. "What? Are you celibate or something?"

"No. I'm just not going to drop my panties for the first handsome man in an Italian suit who thinks I'm pretty. You have to work for these cookies. Nice suit by the way. Who is the designer?"

"It's custom made by an Italian tailor from Miami. How long are we talking?"

"Um, ninety days, give or take a few days. I have to run a background check on you, get your health records, do a credit check and oh yeah check your criminal record."

Mykal fell back in his chair and just stared at the gorgeous woman in front of him. He shook his head in disbelief. "It's funny... The entire time we've been sitting here I've been trying to figure out your flaw. You were just too perfect to believe. What's fun is, the whole time your flaw has been flying like an American flag over your head for the world to see the whole time. I was just too mesmerized by your stunning beauty to notice it."

"So, what it is? What's my flaw?"

"What you don't know?"

Suniya shrugged her shoulders indicating that she didn't have a clue. "Nope!"

"You're crazy! That's your flaw and it as big and as wide and as grand as the damn Grand Canyon! You are crazy!" He chuckled. "Oh my damn! I can't believe I invited a Looney Tune character out to lunch!"

"What's so crazy about what I just said? I have been through too much drama to even consider dating a man that I haven't checked out."

"You know what Suniya? I get that! It's obvious that your last man graduated from Clown University with a PhD in buffoonery. Unfortunately, that's just life. Honestly, if I knew who he was I'd go and plant my size twelve dress shoe up his Simple Jack, sorry ass for hurting you so badly. But, I will not pay for his mistake. I have absolutely no problem with you running every report known to man on me, because I am a good man, a responsible man, a healthy man and my record is squeaky clean. But and there is a big but at the end of that statement… But I will not wait for three months to make love to the woman I'm dating. No, no and hell no! I will not do it. I am a grown man with grown man urges and grown man needs. Trust me within that ninety days I will fuck something, it may not be you… And it won't just be my hand… But you better believe I will have sex with a woman…. At that point you and I will park our happy asses in the friends forever, don't ever touch me zone." He vented. "Seriously, please tell me you're joking about this!"

"I understand your frustration, but I have to protect me. If I don't no one will. And you're right, my ex did have a PhD in buffoonery and a masters in shenanigans. I'll give you his work address before we leave." She chuckled. "I'm sorry, I really am."

"Don't worry about it, it's cool. I'm glad you just put it out there early in the game before I wasted my time spoiling you rotten. I could use some more female friends." Mykal laughed with her. "Yes and I will be needing Bozo's information before we leave, because I'm going to break my foot off in his stupid ass for ruining my chances with you."

"Why does it have to be ruined? Just give it a shot, it might not be that bad." She smiled hoping Mykal would reconsider.

"Suniya, if I told you I would wait for ninety days to be with you I'd just be lying to both of us. Then I'd be no better than any one of the previous jokers and jesters you've trusted. I know me and I know I loved sex too much to even think that I can go ninety days without it and not be in a damn coma."

Suniya poked her lips out to indicate that she was sad. "Aw, that's so unfortunate. I hope in the coming days you'll reconsider."

"Mykal smiled. "I really like you, Suniya. I don't want to start off a relationship lying to you. I'm sorry, but it just won't work."

"Okay, I understand. So now what?"

"Now we have lunch. I'm starving, what about you?"

Mykal summoned their waitress and they ordered the food. They spent the next hour and a half laughing and talking about everything from politics to nail polish. Suniya liked Mykal and she was sad he wasn't willing to put in the effort to date her. She was disappointed, but respected his honesty.

Chapter 12

After Mykal came in with his crew to have them fitted for overcoats Suniya could not stop thinking about him. Mykal Roman was just the kind of man that Suniya was looking for. Hell, he was exactly the type of man Sissy wanted her to date. He was charismatic, sexy, and successful. Most importantly, he was honest.

Mykal hardly looked at her while he was at her shop that day. He spent the bulk of his time on the phone. The moment the order was placed he politely said good bye. Suniya found herself wondering if he had moved on to another woman. It had only been a day, but things move quickly in Atlanta.

Suniya knew that there were women out there who would have slept with Mykal right after their lunch day. Her two sales associates said she was a fool. They both agreed that they would have fucked him in the stock room the day they met him.

She had to consider that Mykal was right, in essence she was making him pay for Tyreese's mistakes. It pissed her off to think that she slept with his sorry as on the third date and she expects Mykal to wait for ninety long and hard days. The more she thought about it the sillier it sound. She hoped she didn't make the wrong decision and missed out on a chance to get to know an incredible man.

At this particular point it had been a week since Suniya last saw Mykal. She could not get her mind off of him. Her mind rehearsed their brief encounters over and over again. Suniya had become obsessed with him. Every idle moment she had was spent thinking about him. At the store she created new and inventive ways to drop his name in a conversation whenever she was with Dani and Jaye.

She dropped his name so much they had grown sick of him and Suniya. They threatened to call Mykal and tell him that Suniya was madly in love with him, if she mentioned his name one more time. Suniya tried to stop, but his name just kept leaping out of her mouth like a damn bull frog.

"Did you see the new cashmere sweaters that just arrived? Mykal would look incredible in that cream colored one on the mannequin."

Dani looked at Jaye and rolled her eyes. She had officially had it. "Yelp, he sure would. Too bad he'll never see it, because somebody Miss Polly Purepussy ass ran him away."

"What?" Suniya asked shocked at Dani's observation.

"Look! I know you're my boss but I have something to say." Jaye stared Suniya dead in her eye and announce.

"What, you agree with Dani?" Suniya asked confused by the confrontation.

"Yes I do, but what I wanted to say was... You're stupid!" She responded. "No! I take that back. You're dumb as hell!"

"I'm sorry, but she's right, Suniya." Dani cosigned.

"Why am I stupid?"

"You let that good man walk right out of your life because you want to play pussy games." Jaye responded. "Now, we have to pay for it. Just admit you're obsessed with him. Pick up the phone and get him back, beg if you have to!"

"She's right again. Suniya, I understand you're trying not to protect your heart, but do you seriously think that a man is going to forego pussy for ninety days just to date you? A man is a man and a man has to get some, from some were, anywhere. If you're not putting out, then he's going to tip out! It's a law of nature, everybody knows that!"

"Why am I wrong? I needed time to thoroughly check him out. That's why I have a ninety day rule."

"Really? I could tell in your eyes after ninety seconds that you wanted that man to break his dick off at the base inside of you. So, cut the bullshit Suniya." Jaye challenged. "You're falling for him. Don't let him go because you want to play juvenile mind games and try to control him."

"I never said I didn't like Mykal."

"Great, here's the phone call him." Dani said as she handed Suniya the store phone.

"Forget that! The order of coats came in today, hand deliver them. With any luck Mykal will be there. If he is then talk to him and get him to go out with you."

"Jaye, he's not going to do that. Unfortunately, I think that ship has already sailed." Suniya sighed.

"Then swim out to sea or call it back to port to pick your little ass up! I swear, if I here Mykal Roman's name casually drop out of your mouth, one more time, I'm going to quit on the spot."

"Me too!" Dani chimed in. "so, what's it going to be Suniya?"

~*~*~

Less than an hour later Suniya found herself at Mykal's office. She knew he said he owned his own transportation business but she never expected such an elaborate set up. His office, grounds and organization were all huge. She couldn't believe it all belonged to him. It was obvious that Mykal was a very successful man. Now, Suniya had to make it obvious to Mykal that she wanted him to be her man.

"Mr. Roman, you have a visitor." Mykal's secretary announced.

Mykal looked up from the contract he was reviewing. "I didn't realize I had an appointment."

"You don't sir. It's the young lady from Gentlemen's Essential boutique. She stopped by to deliver the overcoats you ordered for the drivers."

Mykal's interest peaked instantly. Until that second he was half- ass listening to Carolyn. "What's her name?"

"Suniya, Ms. Suniya Simmons. Should I tell her you're busy?"

"No. It's okay. I have a few minutes. Please show her in."

It was no surprise to Mykal when his dick stirred in his pants at the sound of Suniya's name. Mykal's dick went on ready, red alert every single time she crossed his mind.

Honestly, Mykal hated it. He hated thinking about Suniya, hated wanting Suniya and he hated it when his dick ached for Suniya. "Fuck! Why does this woman have to be so damn crazy?" He groaned beneath his breath as he adjusted his dick in his pants. "Behave! Unless you want to go ninety days without pussy I suggest you fall in love with somebody else," He warned it.

There was a light knock at the door.

"Come in, it's open." He responded.

"Hi, remember me?" Suniya smiled as she peeped in.

"I never forget a crazy person. Come on and have a seat." He chuckled.

"I'll let your crazy person joke go since you're so handsomely dressed in your European suit."

"Thank. You look beautiful."

"Thank you, and if you noticed I'm not wearing pink, just in case you would like to address the pink elephant in the room." She giggled.

"What pink elephant would that be?" Mykal asked puzzled.

Suniya laughed. "Apparently the one I rode into your office unannounced on."

Mykal's dimpled smile quickly assured her it was okay. "Don't worry about that. Actually, it's nice to see you again."

"Really?"

"Yeah. I've been thinking about calling you, but I figured there was no need of wasting either of our time. So, I didn't."

"Yeah, about that… Is there any way we can scratch our previous conversation and start from scratch?"

Mykal looked intrigued. "So when you're talking previous conversation are we talking in particular about the no sex for ninety day conversation? Is that the conversation you'd like to etch out?"

"The whole thing, all of it! I was off the reservation and off my meds and I had no clue what was spilling out of my mind."

Mykal could not believe his ears. It was as if his prayers had been answered. Falling back into his high back, tufted leather chair he sighed a breath of relief. "Wow! Now, that's the best news I had all day."

"Yeah?"

"Definitely! Look, I want you to know that I thought long and hard about your demand, but in the end I knew I couldn't pull it off without disappointing you. I just want to be honest with you."

"Mykal, it's okay. My demands were unreasonable and you were right, I was penalizing you for something someone else did to me and that wasn't fair. I realize that now."

"I have something for you."

"What is it?"

Mykal reached in his draw and pulled out an unsealed FedEx document envelope. It was addressed to Suniya at Gentlemen's Quarters. "Here you go."

Suniya took the envelope and pulled the documents out. "What are these? I don't understand."

"You wanted to check all of my records to make sure I was suitable to date you. So, I had copies made of everything you wanted to look at. I was going to send them to you to speed up the process to about ten days or so."

Suniya was floored. She jumped up, ran around the desk and through herself into Mykal's arms. Before he could protest he mouth covered his in a searing hot kiss. Mykal pulled her into his lap and deepened the kiss.

They kissed for a long breath before the sound of ringing phones reminded Mykal were he was. Reluctantly pulling away he kissed her gently on the lips before setting her free. "Sorry, I got a little carried away.

"Suniya giggled. "No, I'm afraid that was all me. Look I'd better let you get back to work. This place is phenomenal, by the way."

"Thank you! I've been really blessed."

"Yes, I must say you have been. So, Mr. Roman if you don't have any plans I'd like to invite you over to my house to night for dinner and a movie."

"What's the movie?"

"Whatever you pick up from the video store. I'll take care of dinner. You get to select the movie."

"Great! Sounds like a plan. I'll be there at seven."

Suniya pulled one of her business cards from her wallet and scribbled her address and home number on the back of it. "I can't wait." She smiled as she gave it to Mykal.

Mykal stood up and took the card from her outstretched hand. "In that case I'll be there at six."

A smile as bright as sunrise spread across Suniya's face. "Mission accomplished." She thought to herself.

CHAPTER 13

Suniya slowly closed her eyes as Mykal's fingers trailed gently along the length of her shoulders. Then they crawled all over Suniya's back like an agile spider. Mykal had magic hands. He seemed to know what to do and when to do it to melt a woman's panties off. His touch was like a feather blowing gently across Suniya's elegant back, lightly caressing her skin, but at the same time, not touching it.

They had been officially dating for two weeks at this point. Suniya was shocked, Mykal had made absolutely no moves to taste her cookies until tonight. He was a perfect gentleman, but Suniya was finding it difficult to remain a lady in his presence. She welcome his seductive advances and prayed that tonight was the night they'd take their relationship to new heights.

Mykal was all over her, heating her body from within. His expensive cologne assaulted her nostrils and she shuddered slightly. Suniya's skin prickled with goose- bumps and a soft whimper escaped her lips. Mykal's hand had now moved beneath her tank top, down to the flat of her back and then on down to the lush swell of her perfect ass. Without warning his lips had taken the place of his large hands on her shoulders, kissing her delicately while he methodically kneaded the flesh of her derrière through her short, shorts with precision.

Mykal's weight gently forced Suniya onto her stomach on the sofa. Moving quickly, he removed her shorts and panties and spread Suniya's legs apart. Next he began to lightly caress her hot spot, her inner thighs. His other hand slipped beneath her top and caressed her round breast. Grasping the nipple, Mykal squeezed it hard. Suniya winced with pain, but immediately felt a tingling jolt of pleasure travel up her spine causing her to gasp with pleasure. He smiled as she groaned sweetly.

Abandoning her nipple, Mykal used both hands to separate the soft, round mounds of Suniya's ass. The small puckered opening of Suniya's asshole opened and closed with the contractions of her muscles. It momentarily hypnotized him. Dipping his head between her cheeks, Mykal began to leisurely lick up and down the crack of Suniya's ass. She shuddered with delight at the feeling of Mykal's thick, wet tongue. Suddenly, his tongue was at Suniya's anus, prying its way inside.

Suniya's body quaked with desire as his tongue continued to drive her mad. She moaned and groaned softly as passion coursed through her body like an electric current. The ecstasy that Mykal's tongue sliding back and forth inside her asshole was giving her numbed her brain and clouded her consciousness. As he continued to fuck her ass with his tongue, Mykal's fingers located her swollen pussy. Hot cream was oozed controllably from her tight slit and he knew that Suniya was ready for anything.

Suniya squirmed in ecstasy as she felt two thick fingers slide deep into her pussy. It felt like a slender dick stuffing her pussy, in rhythm with Mykal's tongue in her anus. Suniya's pussy swallowed hard and engulfed the fingers. Her juices flowed freely from her tight slit, over his hand and down her thighs, soaking the sofa cushion beneath her. Suniya's body writhed back and forward on the sofa as waves of pleasure crashed against her bringing her closer and closer to an epic orgasm.

Mykal's tongue and fingers were relentless. Suniya's body felt as if it would explode if his tongue made one more pass in and out of her asshole. Arching her back, she threw Mykal off balance and in a second she landed on top of him in the sixty-nine position. Her dripping wet pussy pressed against

Mykal's hungry mouth. He sucked her entire shaved mound in his mouth in one gulp.

Suniya found herself face to face with his humongous bulge. Her nervous fingers worked frantically to unbuckle his pants and free his hard, menacing dick. Unzipping him quickly she wrestled the one eyed serpent from its lair and stroked it firmly to soothe it. Her mouth was now one delectable lick from Mykal's thick, juicy, ten inch dick.

Need and greed consumed her. With a wild lustful growl, she sucked its bulging head into her warm, moist mouth. Mykal's clenched his fists and groan into her pussy as his dick slowly disappeared into the depths of her mouth. Animalistic grunts and growls of lust filtered into the room as they gorged themselves on each other's passion fruit. The warm saliva leaked from their hungry, slurping, licking, sucking, mouths. They were famished and they couldn't seem to get enough.

Suniya spread her thighs wider to accommodate Mykal's head as he continued to suck and lick the hot flesh of her twat. Her head swooned as she sucked harder and harder on his huge dick as her pussy was being feverishly lapped by Mykal's slithering tongue. Never had she enjoyed such pleasure.

Somehow, this delicious man had succeeded in driving Suniya completely insane with lust and desire. Suniya never fathomed her sexual equal existed, but there he was between her tone thighs, eating her pussy like it was a homemade peach cobbler.

Mykal's cunnilingual skills were unmatched. As he feasted on Suniya's pussy, he would occasionally ran his tongue roughly along the entire length of her bottom, from creamy pussy to juicy asshole. Then he'd gnaw on her erect, throbbing clit with the sharp fangs of his teeth. After that he'd roll his tongue around the entrance of her oozing pussy and then flick it around the sides of her vaginal walls. Just for good measure he'd then wet Suniya's asshole with saliva and promptly jam two fingers deep into her anus.

Needless to say, Suniya was vacationing on the shores of paradise. She grunted and gyrated on his hand as she sucked his dick further to the back of her greedy mouth. Mykal was driving her mad. Her release unexpectedly stormed in and slapped her silly. Loud, primitive gasps, squawks and grunts came from her throat. Suniya screeched a long string of obscenities, as she struggled against her raging climax.

"Oh shit! I'm coming... I'm coming! Eat me... Eat that damn pussy! F-u-c-k! I'm coming!" She screamed at the top of her lungs.

Mykal sucked her clit deep into his mouth and began to fuck her asshole with his fingers extra hard and extra fast. He knew she was coming hard and he wanted her to remember her orgasm for as long as she breathed. Harder and harder he finger fucked in and out of Suniya's ass, as he sucked the skin off of clit and licked her swollen, juicy pussy.

Suniya was hotter than a bitch in heat as she spontaneously combusted and burned into tiny bits of ash right in his arms. His dick was raging hard and still lodged in the back of her throat as she suddenly experienced her second climax. She had to get that delectable dick inside of her.

Snatching her snatch from his grasp she quickly mounted his throbbing dick. The large mushroom head threatened to split her tight pussy apart, but Suniya didn't give a good damn. Slamming down hard she took his full length in one giant thrust as her orgasm punched her repeatedly in the face as if it was a speed bag.

"Oh f-u-c-k yeah! Handle that fuckin dick, girl!" Mykal growled as his eyes rolled around in his head like a loose bag of marbles. "Ah fuck me! Fuck me!" He grunted and groaned as Suniya rode him hard, reverse cowgirl style. Grabbing her round ass Mykal arched his back, thrust his ass forward and slammed his diamond hard, throbbing dick into her steaming hot pussy completely raw. "F-u-c-k! This feels so fuckin good! Fucking ride that fucking hard dick!"

Suddenly, Mykal screamed out like a frightened toddler as the spasms of his epic climax ripped through his body as quick as a Texas tornado on an open range. Screaming, cussing, yelling and growling intangible obscenities he drenched the walls of Suniya's pussy with his hot, thick love cream.

Suniya's body continued to buck hard riding that humongous, monster of a dick until it went limp. She was determined to get her third orgasm in before Mykal lost his erection. She was in the zone, riding and grinding her hungry pussy against Mykal's hard dick as if the world would end if she stopped. Suniya refused to stop until her body erupted with its third climax. She wanted it. She needed it and she was hell bent on getting it.

"Don't you dare quit on me! Fuck this pussy! Fuck it until I come! You wanted this good pussy, now show me you know how to fuck it!" She screamed and Mykal obeyed.

Suddenly, Suniya felt as if the air was being sucked from her lungs as she struggled to catch her breath. She could feel the tension build and build in her body as she neared her goal. Yet her climax seemed so far off. Without warning her release rolled up her back from her ass and choked the shit out of her. She couldn't move, she couldn't scream and she couldn't breathe, and then it happened.

The dark room caved in on her and a kaleidoscope of bright lights and vivid colors appeared to flash all around her body. Everything went red and Suniya's body exploded into crushed pixie dust. The massive contractions of the walls of her pussy felt like they were turning her body inside out. Screams of ecstasy erupted from her throat and tears ran down her face as the convulsions of her released smacked her into a euphoric state.

Mykal felt her body go limp and quickly gathered her in his massive arms and held her twitching body close. He closed his eyes and sighed as he felt the warm ocean of pussy juice spew from her slit onto the mat of hair above his semi- flaccid dick. In awe of this incredible woman he held her tight and they drifted off to sleep.

CHAPTER 14

The next morning Suniya woke up in Mykal's arms. She couldn't believe they slept the night away in each other's arm. Mykal was still knocked out. Suniya smiled, he had her on the ropes last night, but in the end she put his ass in a coma. Snuggling back in his arms she savored her victory.

Mykal was fine as refined Arabian sand. She watched him for a while as he slept, he looked so peaceful. He was sound asleep. Just as she thought about waking him up for another round something odd caught her eye.

Mykal was not wearing a condom. "Where the hell did it go?" Suniya mumbled to herself as she looked around.

Examining his cum encrusted dick closer it hit her like a frozen sack of quarters. She mounted him before he had the chance to strap up!

"Oh my God!" She panicked and screamed. Slapping him hard on his chest to arouse him she yelled. "Did you come in me?"

Mykal was groggy and disoriented and had no idea what was going on. "What?" He managed. "What's wrong?"

Hopping up from the sofa Suniya stuck her hand in between her legs into her cum soaked pussy and produced body fluids on her fingers for him to see. "Please do not tell me that this is semen! Is it? Mykal is it semen?" She hysterically yelled.

Finally, Mykal sat up on the sofa to see what was wrong with her. "Baby, calm down. What's going on?"

Suniya, held her hands up in surrender. She took several deep breaths and tried to calm down, but she couldn't. Suniya paced back and forth like a caged panther. She did not speak until she collected her thoughts. "Mykal, did you use a condom last night when we had sex?"

Mykal looked puzzled. "I was going to but…"

"Oh fuckin hell no! But what? What the fuck were you thinking? You came inside of me without a damn condom? Seriously, Mykal? Why would you do that?" She stomped and yelled and screamed at the top of her lungs as she pulled at her hair like a crazy person. "Who the fuck does that?"

"What? Suniya! You jumped on me while we were in the middle of 69. You hopped on my dick raw. Calm down. I don't have anything. I'm clean, you saw my medical records, for God's sake. The world will not come to an end because you had sex one time without a damn condom!"

Wrong answer. Suniya suddenly remembered that in fact it was all her doing. The problem was that Suniya had just received her birth control shot and was not supposed to have unprotected sex for at least a week. It had only been two days.

"You idiot! I didn't have birth control! Remember?" She screeched.

"You told me you had got the shot!" Mykal retorted.

"Yeah, I did, but I was supposed to use condoms for the first seven days as a backup." She retaliated. "I thought you knew that!"

Now, Mykal was frightened, but pissed. "Two questions... How the fuck was I supposed to know that bullshit? And why in the hell did you hop on my damn dick like you were a professional rodeo clown?" He snapped back. "F-u-c-k! This is bullshit!"

Wrong question, wrong tone, wrong attitude and wrong fucking response! Suniya was furious and immediately saw crimson red. She grabbed Mykal's clothes and shoes and threw them out the front door onto the porch. Then she returned to the family room, grabbed Mykal's big ass by the ankles and snatched him off the couch. His head hit the floor with a loud, dull thump. He was momentarily dazed and confused. Then Suniya drug his butt naked ass through the house, out the front door and on to the porch. She then went back into her house, slammed the door and then locked it.

Now, the same sack of frozen quarters that slapped Suniya rebounded and slapped Mykal in the face as well. He had no damn clue what had just happened. Hell, he couldn't figure out how that tiny woman was strong enough to drag his two hundred and twenty five pound ass off her couch and out of her house.

Stunned, bewildered and confused he rang the doorbell. "Suniya, open the door! Stop playing!"

Mykal was so disoriented he didn't even realize that he was outside, in a suburban middleclass neighborhood, ass out, butt crack naked. Well, that is until a car drove by and blasted the horn at him.

Grabbing his clothes in front of him, Mykal snatched his shoes and ducked behind a large tree in Suniya's front yard. There he slipped on his jeans and shoes. Fishing his car keys from his pocket he made a mad dash for his car.

You would have thought Mykal drove race cars for NASCAR, the way he peeled out of Suniya's driveway. Now he was wide awake, fully alert and he was officially fucking pissed!

"What the Fuck just happened?" He screamed at the top of his lungs as he made his way to the highway to head home.

Driving like a maniac he blew through the residential neighborhood in his Porsche at seventy miles an hour. It was a miracle he made it out of there without a ticket. "You knew this chick was nuttier than a fucking bag of Snickers bar! Why the fuck did you fuck her! She's right! You're a fucking idiot, Mykal Roman!" He screamed at himself.

CHAPTER 15

Every blood vessel in Suniya's body coursed with adrenalin. She was drunk from its affect. Crazed she yelled and screamed and tugged at her hair as she paced over her home trying to figure out what just happened.

One minute she was lying in her king's arm and the next she was dragging him through her living room and tossing his naked ass out on her front porch. Not only was Mykal naked, but she was naked as well.

"Oh my God! What must my neighbors think? Did anyone see me? Please do not tell me that Sade nosy ass saw us. OMG! Someone please tell me that nobody saw my naked ass throw Mykal's big naked ass out of my house like a mad woman!" She vented as she continued to pace. "How the hell did I even get the strength to do that? Of course someone saw you dumb ass! Oh my God, I'm going to have to move! Hell, I may even have to leave Atlanta! Checked that... They have YouTube and Boobtube now... I'll have to move to a remote village in Mexico to rid myself of this shame! Way to go

Suniya! Way to ruin your life and embarrass yourself in the process!"

From the outside looking in, Suniya appeared to be as crazy as a bedbug in heat as she paced the floor talking to herself. Occasionally she'd grabbed her long her as if she was trying to pull it out by the roots and then she'd run in circles and scream. Yelp, at this point she was as nutty as a sack on chimp balls.

A flood of emotions swarmed her brain as she tried to make sense of it all. She tried to process the scenario over and over again, but it just didn't add up. For the life of her Suniya could not figure out where her super human power emerged from.

"Mykal, must really think I'm a crazy Looney Tune now. That's where my strength came from... Everybody knows that crazy people are super strong and cocky. I guess that's it... I'm as crazy as hell! It's official, Suniya Simmons has gone coo-coo for chocolate flavored Co-Co Puffs with bananas over a damn dick!" She mindlessly ranted.

Initially Suniya was furious at Mykal, that's why she threw him out. Now, her gears shifted and she started to become concerned. She remembered the sound his head made when it hit the floor after she snatched him off her couch. She prayed he didn't have head trauma.

"Lord, please let him be alright! I wasn't trying to kill him I just had to get him out my damn house before I did!"

Honestly, she realized that the whole condom missing in action fiasco was her own damn fault. The dick was just so good and she was just so excited. She hopped on it like she was mounting a stallion and she rode Mykal like he was a prize winning thoroughbred. Suniya had to admit it was the ride of her life.

"Idiot! Best dick you ever had and you had to fuck it up by being overzealous!" She screamed at herself as she caught the reflection of herself in the large wall mirror in her foyer.

Now, Suniya's reaction to Mykal earlier stemmed from her maddening fear of getting pregnant. All of her life she was careful with her health, body and her birth control. The thought of being a single, unwed mom haunted her relentlessly. It was drilled into her sub consciousness to always use protection. Sissy and her grandmother both taught her to never trust a man to protect her from disease and pregnancy.

They taught her that condoms were the woman's responsibility, not the man's. Towards that end Suniya would either watch the man sheath his dick with a condom or she'd do it herself. She never ever took chances and she never made exceptions. So, what happened last night baffled her.

The situation wouldn't have been so serious and escalated so quickly if the risk of pregnancy wasn't so high. Suniya was on a break from dick. So, she took a brief break from birth control while she was celibate. After all, she had instituted her ninety days law, so she'd have plenty of time to restart her birth control regimen. Suniya never fathomed she'd meet a man that would take her so quickly. Then Mykal Roman waltzed into her life and broke all of her rules.

She probably would have had an entirely different response if the fear of an unwanted pregnancy was not so deeply engrained into her DNA. Faced with the real possibility that this one slip up could lead to an unplanned pregnancy and single parenthood, Suniya burst into tears. Throwing her nude frame on her white Victorian sofa, she sobbed like a toddler who lost their pacifier.

CHAPTER 16

Still furious, Mykal rushed into his door and headed straight for his bar. Grabbing a glass he poured himself a double shot of Scotch, downed it and then poured another. He swallowed hard as the single- malt whiskey slid down his throat and quickly calmed his nerves.

It was Saturday and barring any unforeseen catastrophe, Michael was off until Monday. The plan for the day was to spend it with Suniya visiting antique shops. She was young, but for some reason loved and collected antiques. Mykal, had always been fascinated by shows like Antique Road show, so they agreed to go antiquing.

"Suniya! Crazy ass Suniya!" He breathed as he took a sip of his second glass of Scotch.

Just the thought of her name made his blood boil hot and not in a good way. He had never been so humiliated in his entire life. Nor had he ever been so wrongfully accused. Mykal did nothing wrong and he knew it.

Yet Suniya treated him like he had just shot a load of every sexually transmitted disease non to man, into her with malice. Mykal had no idea she wasn't on birth control, or he would have stopped her, so he thought. The truth of the matter they were both so caught up in the moment neither of them were thinking straight.

"This is bullshit!" He muttered. "I did nothing wrong. The irony of the matter is that she's probably not even pregnant!" Then the thought hit him, "What if she was?"

Mykal downed the remainder of the whiskey and played with the rim of the glass as he considered the possibilities. Other than the fact that Suniya, in his mind, was insane; he'd love to have a baby by her. She's intelligent, beautiful, spiritually grounded and an all- around good person. She'd make an excellent mom.

He chuckled. "The problem is that woman is as crazy as a maniac on crack." Pondering the issue further, he was drawn back to reality by the security buzzer which indicated someone was at the front door of his condo building. "Please do not let this be this crazy lady at my damn condo."

Checking the screen on the security screen he was relieved to discover that it was Victoria. He smiled as he hit the buzzer to let her in.

Within moments Victoria walked in dressed in a sexy dress that reminded Mykal exactly why they were still friends after all these years. She went to greet him with a kiss on the lips, as she routinely did, but Mykal stopped her. The taste of Suniya's pussy was still on his lips.

"Morning breath... I just got up." He lied.

"Okay... If you say so." She suspiciously eyed him as she spotted the glass in his hand. "Why are you drinking this time of day? What's going on?"

Mykal rubbed his head. He didn't know how to respond to that question. On the one hand Victoria was his friend, but on the other hand she was also his lover. He'd never mentioned Suniya to her, because he wasn't sure it was going to materialize into something significant. He eyed Victoria as he contemplated telling her. He decided it was the best thing to do, besides he needed to talk to someone.

"I met someone." He breathed.

"Oh, okay! I understand. I didn't mean to stop by unannounced but you weren't answering your phone. I'll go." She nervously babbled thinking that someone was there with Mykal.

"Ah shit! I left my damn phone at crazy's!" He hissed as he patted down his pockets in search of his cell.

Victoria breathed a silent sigh of relief. Making herself at home on the sofa she watched as Mykal franticly searched the pile of clothes he'd discard near the door when he arrived. "Damn it! Where's my phone? And where are my damn draws?"

Victoria immediately erupted in laughter. "What the hell happened to you last night? Look at you! This is just too funny! Who did you sleep with last night? You look like a wild man. You're half dressed, your shoes are on the wrong feet and to top it off you're ranting and raving over some boxer shorts! This is funny as hell. I don't recall ever seeing Mykal Roman this disheveled."

Mykal stopped in mid rant. He had to admit it was funny. Tossing the discarded clothes in a pile back on the floor he joined her on the couch. "I met this crazy ass sales clerk at a clothing store. She was the typical bitter woman, but I pushed past all of that bullshit because I liked her and I wanted to get to know her. So, I asked her out and we went to lunch. At lunch, the very first day I met her mind you, she tells me all of this bullshit about she needed to check my credit and background and health records before she'd even consider dating me."

"Sounds like a whole lot of work for some lack luster pussy." Victoria giggled as she pretended to check her freshly manicured nails for hangnails and flaws.

Mykal gave her the side eyed look. It was obvious that she was jealous. "Who said the pussy was lack luster?" Victoria gave him a little, fuck you smirk. "So anyway... She hits me with the big guns... No damn sex for ninety days!"

"Ouch! That's what we call a deal breaker." Victoria chuckled. "Sorry, go ahead."

"Nah, you're right. It definitely was a deal breaker. I told her I wasn't interested. Long story short, she pursued me, showed up at the office and recanted her ninety day rule."

"I bet you fucked her right then and there, didn't you?"

"What? No! You should know me better than that. I don't fuck where I work and I don't work were I fuck. I don't have a lot of rules, but that's one. Actually, I was a complete gentleman and dated her for a full two weeks."

"So, in the two weeks' time, you didn't notice that she was hiding crazy in the closet?"

No! She was normal, hell she was better than normal. She was looking like a winner and then last night happened."

"What happened last night?"

"Okay, let me ask you this, because I know we don't normal discuss our dates... You're not going to get jealous, right?"

Victoria eyed the handsome man. She really didn't know how she was going to feel. For some odd reason the dynamics of their relationship shifted when they moved to Atlanta. Victoria was feeling things for Mykal she'd never thought she'd feel and admittedly jealousy was one of them. So, she lied.

"No, of course not! Why would I be jealous? We're just friends, right?"

"Just checking. So... I'm feeling this woman in a major way, sexually, emotionally, hell even spiritually and I wanted to take our relationship to the sexual level." He eyes Victoria for a reaction, but she was wearing her stoic face.

"Continue." She casually replied.

"We had a nice dinner, a walk around the neighborhood by the lake and when we got back I made my move. Then we went at it like to hippopotamus in heat."

"What? Did she stopped you mid hump or something... What happened?"

"No we had sex alright… No holes barred, toe cracking sex, leg numbing sex. There was just one problem. In the mist of our enthusiasm, we forgot to use a condom."

"So, what do you know about this girls sexual history? Is she clean or what?" Victoria asked concerned.

"Don't worry, she's clean. She's a good girl, she doesn't sleep around and normally protects herself. We exchanged health records so I know she's disease free. That's not the problem."

Victoria sighed a breath of relief. "Okay, so what's the problem?"

"Problem is she'd been celibate and restarted her birth control regimen after we started dating. She'd taken the birth control shot and was supposed to use condoms as a backup."

Victoria eyed Mykal. She could sense there was more and was determined not to interrupt. Her poker face was still plastered on and Mykal couldn't read what she was thinking, but he sensed she was a tad bit pissed. So, he decided to wrap the story up quick and do damage control as soon as possible.

"So fast forward to the next morning... She wakes up and has an epiphany that we didn't use a condom and she may be at risk of becoming pregnant and she zapped the fuck out. She woke me up ranting and raving and pulling out her hair. Next thing I know she had tossed my butt naked, big dick ass out of her house. I had to get dress behind a tree in her yard. Now, it looks like the psycho probably has my phone, so expect a call any second now." Victoria didn't say a word. She just continued to stare at Mykal as if his nose had magically turned into a unicorn's dick. "Say something Tori. Don't just stare at me like that." Victoria was speechless. "See, I knew I shouldn't have confided all of this nonsense with you. Now, I feel like I just confessed to infidelity to my wife. Tori please... Say something... Anything!"

Victoria pushed her real feelings to the back burner and made light of the matter. She didn't want Mykal to know she was jealous. So she masked her emotions with the performance of a life time. "Bravo! Bravo!" She clapped. "Best story I ever heard." She continued to clap. "Well! I guess congratulations are in order, as well. Apparently, you've just impregnated a crazy bitch!" She laughed. "You wanted a child and look like you're going to get your wish!"

"Stop laughing. None of that is funny. I didn't want a baby that way and certainly not by a schizophrenic maniac with super natural strength and agility. Oh God, please don't let crazy be having a baby." Mykal laughed to keep from crying. "What the hell did I do?"

Victoria laughed with him. She also wanted to cry, but crying wasn't an option. Mykal could never find out that she was falling for him in a big way. They made light of the issue, but her cut told her that Mykal had just knocked this woman and shit just got real!

CHAPTER 17

Mykal and Victoria had a good laugh about the whole thing although deep down they both knew there wasn't a damn thing funny. Both of them were torn up inside for varying reasons. Victoria didn't want to lose Mykal to a pregnant psycho and Mykal didn't want to admit that crazy or not, he'd fallen for Suniya in a big way.

They decided to spend the rest of the day together, hang out and have some fun. Victoria offered to treat Mykal to lunch at his favorite restaurant and he welcomed the distraction. So, headed off to take a much need shower and get dressed.

The warm water hit his body and instantly began to relax Mykal's tense muscles. He closed his eyes and started to lather up with a large natural sea sponge. As he relaxed his mind drifted to the beautiful Suniya and suddenly he found himself with a full on erection. After all she had just put him through, he could believe his dick still responded at the thought of her.

As he gave it a soothing tug it grew even harder and thicker. "Fuck!" He breathed. "This woman has my ass twisted in knots thinking about her crazy ass!"

Pleasuring himself he drifted off to a dimension were the condom incident did not exist. His eyes closed tighter as the hot water of the shower and his strong steady hand magically took his cares away. Anxiety rolled off Mykal like the water which cleansed his body. He sighed as his hand made all his doubts, worries and fears dissipate.

Mykal had a large walk in marble shower which was encased in glass, but didn't have a door. His eyes were closed so he didn't see Victoria as she joined him in the shower. He gasped and then sighed a big breath of appreciation as she replaced his large hand with hers.

She spoke not a word, but went right to work. Positioning herself in front of him she squatted before him and slowly caressed his hard dick. Stroking his engorged manhood from root to tip and back again she helped Mykal forget the events of his trying morning.

Mykal could feel her eyes searching his face for confirmation and approval. He opened his eyes and their eyes met. He touched her face lovingly as he watched her suck his dick into her mouth.

Her mouth was some and welcomed his hard dick with unconditional love. An indescribable blanket of warmth settled over Mykal's spirit as the beautiful Victoria sucked and slurped on his hard dick.

Mykal reached down and effortlessly pulled Victoria up into his muscular arms. Her long legs wrapped themselves around his muscular torso for support. Pinning her back to the marble wall, Mykal kissed her hard and deep. Their tongues danced to an old familiar love song.

Victoria's felt the kiss in her manicured toes. Her body slumped forward onto him in passionate, sweet surrender. Entwining her arms around his neck she held on as Mykal positioned his rock hard, dripping cock at the entrance of her tight pussy. She wanted him so bad she was about to faint with desire.

The thick head of his manhood probed against the tight folds of her hungry pussy as it sought entrance. Victoria's round breasts gleefully bounced as she thrust her body further down Mykal's torso in an attempt to accommodate his giant dick. Mykal met her downward stroke with a powerful upward stroke which allowed his throbbing dick to sink balls to ass deep in Victoria's quivering cunt.

Her body quaked as his thickness filled her completely. Hungry for his dick she met him stroke after stroke as he fucked deeper and deeper into her warm pussy. Pleasure radiated through both of them with each centimeter he sank inside of her as her tight walls milked his thunderous cock.

A long throaty groan escaped from Victoria's lips as she felt her pussy tightening to grasp and squeeze the huge monster thrusting in her womanhood and pummeling her G-spot. The sensation was maddening and somehow felt indecent to feel Mykal plowing her pussy like that after just leaving the arms of another woman. Victoria didn't care. Mykal Roman was more her man than the crazy ladies and she'd be damn if she let him go without a fight.

Victoria's thighs shook uncontrollably as her orgasm began to form in her loins. Her arms tightened around Mykal's neck. She snatched her mouth from his, interrupting their kiss so she could breathe. Her breath was erratic and came in short spurts. Mykal could sense she was about to come.

Mykal grabbed her around the waist tightly and pulled her pelvis down to meet his. With each and every stroke he impaled her pussy on his rampaging cock. Victoria was coming now. She screamed as she grinded her hips down on Mykal's throbbing dick. He continued to ram her using monstrous dick like a giant dildo made specifically her gratification and satisfaction.

"Fuck me! Fuck me hard with big fucking dick!" Victoria screamed as Mykal slammed in and out of her repeatedly.

Mykal didn't need an invitation, because that was exactly what he planned to do. The engorged head of his dick brutally assaulted her G-spot as he went balls deep with every pump. Victoria's whimpering, jerking and flailing only fueled his resolve. Mykal was determined to punch a hole in her back and fuck her silly.

As Victoria came the spasms from her pussy resonated through her vaginal walls forcing them to contract around Mykal's hard cock. The sensation was mind boggling. Moments later he felt his release storm his erotic center and send his body into convulsions. Somehow he managed to fire off ten hard and fast thrusts into her swollen pussy before his climax overtook him and rendered him completely incapacitated.

Seconds later Mykal flooded Victoria's pussy with squirt after squirt of his thick manly seed. Roaring loudly, he wrestled fiercely with the monstrous orgasm that gripped and ripped through his balls. Sampling Victoria lips he held her close as his body continued to tremble from the powerful aftermath of his epic release.

Mykal smiled as he realized his Saturday somehow turned out perfectly.

CHAPTER 18

Two weeks quickly passed by and the itch in Suniya's thong made her obsess over Mykal even more than normal. They had barely begin when they were so abruptly ended by the dreaded condom incident. In retrospect Suniya felt like a fool. She realized she acted like a complete idiot and totally handled the situation wrong. The fact that it really wasn't Mykal's fault made her feel even worse.

Suniya wasn't big on admitting she was wrong. Some would even venture to say she was as stubborn as a castrated bull when it came to accepting blame and apologizing. Raised as an only child and essentially spoiled to believe the world started and stopped on her command, she never learned that it's okay to be wrong and admit fault.

When it came to men, she'd rather be stripped naked, rubbed in butter and left out in a blazing, noonday Mexico sun than accept responsibility for her actions. She was beautiful, sexy and a heel of a lay, so most men caved in long be sure she did. Mykal Roman wasn't most men, in fact he was unlike any man she'd ever encountered.

Mykal was exactly seven years older than Suniya. So, a lot of the little immature tantrums she normally pulled did not affect him. Suniya could not believe he hadn't called her. Hell if nothing else he could have at least made up a lame excuse to stop by her store. She had even sent him a promotional email from the store's email account but he didn't bite.

Desperate, she made an attempt to stalk him on Facebook only to discover he didn't have a Facebook page. However she did find a Facebook page for his transportation company. Cruising through the posts and pictures of this incredibly sex man made her realize that she had fucked up big time.

Suniya picked up the phone to call him, but her message went right to voicemail. She quickly realized that her apology should be done face to face. Mykal was humiliated when she threw him out of her house naked. Racking her brain for an acceptable peace offering Suniya grabbed her purse and headed out the door.

Like it or not Suniya knew she had to make up with Mikal and admit she was wrong. If she was lucky Mykal would forgive her and they could start fresh for the second time. She knew she was running out of second chances, but she was captivated by this man. Suniya had no other choice but to choke down a big slice of humble pie and beg for Mykal's forgiveness.

At this point she'd do or say anything to win him back and rid herself of the annoying ache in her groin. Sex with Mykal was phenomenal and his intimate touch haunted her spirit. She'd never felt this way over a man and it frightened her. Suniya had to know if this feeling that possessed her was strictly about dick or something much deeper. In order to do that she had to finagle away to get back in his arms.

Within an hour she found herself standing outside of Mykal's office holding an antique picnic basket full of Mykal's favorite food and a bottle of his favorite wine. Whispering a silent prayer, Suniya waited for his secretary to announce her.

"Mr. Roman, sorry to interrupt you, but your lunch date is here."

Mykal, looked up at Nan, his secretary, baffled. "Okay... I wasn't aware I had a lunch appointment."

Nan giggled, "You do now. There's a very beautiful woman with a picnic basket waiting patiently to see you."

"Who is it?" Mykal asked realizing that Nan was up to something. "And why are you giggling like a schoolgirl?"

"It's Suniya silly. Who did you think it was?"

Intrigued, Mykal's left brow quickly raised. Slumping back in his chair he sighed. "Wow! Didn't see that one coming." Mykal's mind raced as he mulled over the prospect of seeing Suniya again. Truth be told, he'd missed her, but didn't feel up with to the drama associated with making up.

"So, shall I show her in or are you two going out?"

Mykal through his hands up indicating that he had no clue. "Yeah! I guess... Just show her in, so I can talk to her."

"Okay! Right away." Nan smiled.

Suniya walked into Mykal's office and the air instantly vacated his lungs. She was wearing an elegant, but form fitting red dress that hugged and caressed her curvaceous body. Mykal's dick raised its head and change position. "Ah shit!" Mykal moaned beneath his breath as he stood from behind his desk to greet her.

"Surprise, surprise!" Suniya playfully chirped as she approached him, stopping short of his desk.

"Ms. Suniya Simmons, I must say I'm a little surprised to see you here." He smiled as his eyes slowly raked over her luscious frame and settled on her beautiful face. "You look incredible, as always."

"Thank you." She breathed. "A single woman has to do her best to remain competitive in this world of Divas."

A sexy grin crept across Mykal's face. "I'm sure you have no problem in that arena. So, what can I do for you today?"

Suniya smiled as she held up her picnic basket. "Have lunch with me, I'd like to talk to you for a second."

Mykal sighed deeply. He was nervous. It had been two weeks since there incident and he was afraid Suniya had taken a pregnancy test. With mixed emotions he replied, "Sure! Let's go over here, so we can relax."

"I like that suit. You look very handsome." Suniya, flirted as she followed Mykal to seating area in front of a large picture window. Mykal smiled and offered her a seat. She joined him on the sofa and place her picnic basket on the large coffee table. "I hope you're hungry, because I brought all of your favorites."

Mykal chuckled. "Suniya, please tell me you have no intentions of poisoning your baby daddy for revenge."

Suniya laughed. "What? I'm not pregnant! I took a home pregnancy test a week ago, I'm fine. I'm here to apologize."

"Apologize for what?" Mykal knew what she was referring to, but he was not going to let her off the hook so easily.

"Well, apparently there was this escaped lunatic who escaped from Skyland Trails Mental Institution and was masquerading as me."

"Oh really? So, was she the one who..." Mykal played along.

"Yes, she was the one who drug you out of my house and tossed you on the porch naked. That's why she was so strong, she's crazy as hell!"

Mykal chuckled. "Yeah! I'll agree with you there. My question was, is she the one who made love to me and put me into a coma when she was finished? If so, I don't give a damn how crazy she is I want to see her again!"

Suniya grimaced. "Yeah, probably so."

"Wow!" Mykal licked his lips and seductively eyed the beautiful woman. There was no denying the fact that he was mind numbingly attracted to Suniya. Every cell in his body screamed for him to throw her down on that couch and fuck her until she was ruin for all other men. "Now, that chick was crazy as Mexican jumping beans, but she was sexy as hell! Ironically, she looked just like you, but without the clothes. Where did you say they locked here up? I need to pay her a visit."

"Mykal, I am so sorry about that morning. I was so frightened that I might become pregnant I temporarily lost my mind. Look, I know you think I have issues, and you're probably right... But I really like you and I would an opportunity to prove to you that I'm sane. Okay? I know it may be a lot to ask, but if you do I promise I'll put crazy on hold. Okay?"

A sexy, devilish grin tugged at the corners of Mykal's mouth. His dick stirred in his pants at the thought of a round of makeup sex. Hell, he could say no even if he wanted to. "Alright, apology accepted. So, do you have any desert in your basket?"

Suniya looked in the picnic basket and pulled out a big slice of triple chocolate, chocolate cake. "Yeah, here you go."

"Actually, I had something a little more succulent in mind."

Mykal took the cake from her outstretched hand and set it down on a side table. Without another word he pulled Suniya into his arms. Their eyes met briefly. Suniya's breasts pressed against his chest. She wanted Mykal so bad they burned with lust.

His sexy brown eyes continued to stare at her with the faraway look of a man who was about to take a giant leap of faith. He longed for Suniya like no other woman he'd ever known. Sane or insane he didn't care. He was determined to ride her until she told him to stop.

Suniya shortened the distance between their mouths and tilted her head slightly, indicating that she desired to be kissed. Mykal took her cue and moved in to kiss her, stopping a less than a millimeter from her full inviting lips. He wasn't sure why he hesitated.

"Suniya, I want to take things slow with you. I really do, but I'm not sure if I can. I know you wanted to keep things light."

"Mykal, what do I know?"

"I think you're right. Let's take a breath and slow things down a bit. It will help us avoid misunderstandings and blow ups like we had in the past. Okay?"

Nodding her head slowly, Suniya reluctantly agreed. She didn't want to slow down and she regretted ever indicating that she did. Mykal was it for her. She didn't want to see anyone else. It saddened her to think that Mykal wanted the freedom to date other women. Unfortunately, it was her bed of nails, she created it and she'd have to lie in it, well until she could convince Mykal she was right for him.

"Okay." She mumbled as she seized the opportunity to kiss him.

Every fiber of his being told Mykal to make a clean break and walk away. However, every cell in his body screamed for him to mount her right there and break his dick off in her. It was a difficult decision, a virtual coin toss would decide his fate. Staring into her eyes and feeding off her need he made his decision. So, he walked over to his desk, picked up the phone and called his secretary. "Nan hold all of my calls until further notice."

"No problem Mr. Roman." She smiled to herself.

CHAPTER 19

Mykal had every intention of allowing Suniya to leave his office without being fucked, but his dick had other plans. Syphoning the blood from his brain as it stiffened to a rigidity reserved for steel, his big, bold dick took over his body and immediately started giving orders.

"Bend over this chair and stick that fine ass up in the air for me!" His sultry voice commanded as he leaned against the front of his desk with his legs crossed at the ankles. Suniya complied. Mykal smiled as he admired Suniya's round ass as it poked high in the air. "Now, lift your dress up so I can see that onion booty, I've been craving for two weeks.

Suniya was shocked but she did exactly as she was told. She wanted and needed to be told what to do. Somehow it made her feel like less of a slut if she was commanded to do it, even though she wanted to. She didn't quite know why, but it also heightened her arousal when a man like Mykal took control.

Straightening up a bit, she lifted the hem of her clingy red dress so it rested above her waist. She was wearing a red lace thong. Mykal unconsciously rubbed his dick through his pants as he eyed his prize. He nodded for her to resume her position over the chair.

Suniya immediately bent over the armchair and held on to the arms for support. She was a ball of emotions. She was excited, frightened and nervous all at the same time.

"Bend over further. I want that ass high in the air." Mykal's sexy voice ordered in a low seductive tone.

Suniya groaned as her pussy swallowed hard in anticipation. Her legs trembled and her knees grew weak. She wanted him so badly she could hardly breathe, let alone stand. Spreading her legs a little wider for leverage she bent further over and stuck her ass out as far as she possibly could.

Mykal eyed her as she watched him remove his wallet from his pants pocket. Searching through it he produced a condom. Playfully he held it up for her to see and then placed it beside him on the desk.

He stood up and removed his suit jacket and walked around his desk and hung it on the back of his chair. Then he removed his tie and shirt and neatly draped them over one arm of the chair. Dressed only in his wife- beater T- shirt and trousers he returned to the front of his desk.

Unbuckling his belt and undoing zipper he dropped his pants and boxers together, so that hung just below his tight muscular ass. Suniya's eyes locked on his veiny dick. It appeared angry as it sprung to freedom.

Mykal grasped it firmly and stroked it gently to calm it. Removing the condom with one hand he expertly sheathed his twitching dick. Suniya's eyes widened in anticipation as he approached and moved behind her. Her neck craned around to see what he was doing back there.

"Mykal, I…"

"Silence! No talking!" He sternly commanded and she immediately shut up.

Pressing his rigid cock against her ass, he reached around to caress her breasts through the fabric of her dress. Suniya gasped as he kneaded her flesh as if it was bread dough. With his other hand he guided his hard dick along the slit of her wet pussy.

"Oh my God! Please hurry up and fuck me with that big damn dick! I can't stand this another second!" Suniya groaned and begged as her need swelled and boiled out of her throat in the form of dirty talk.

Mykal smiled, but warned. "I said silence!"

Suniya gripped the arms of the chair so tightly the blood left her knuckles and they appeared pale. Mykal knew she was less than a clit lick away from an orgasm. Removing her thong, he dropped to his knees and sucked her swollen clit into his mouth.

The sensation was unexpected and overpowering. Forbidden to speak Suniya stomped her right foot repeated. Mykal recognized that her climax was at hand. Giving her three hard licks from her clit to her asshole he orchestrated her release.

Stomping both feet, Suniya swallowed her screams as she experienced a mind boggling orgasm. Whimpering and flailing and gyrating against Mykal's greedy mouth she came hard and fast. Gripping the arms of the chair with all her might she almost snapped the wooden arms off.

Mykal wasted no time. He sprang to his feet, positioned his throbbing dick against her quivering pussy and slammed into her balls deep. The force it placed on her clit almost made her come again. Suniya's heart raced and her blood surged as Mykal drove his big stiff dick into her drooling pussy repeatedly.

"Shit, your pussy is so damn tight!" he hissed as hammered into her G-spot.

Close to another catastrophic release, Suniya snorted, "Silence! No talking!"

A devious grin slid quickly across Mykal's handsome face as he got the message. Suniya Simmons was not an easy woman to tame. Following her command he went to work to make sure she got the proper fuck she sought.

Mykal moved his hips back and forth like a well-engineered piston as he plunged his dick deeper and deeper into her soaking wet koochie. Her orgasm had created the perfect environment for Mykal's, extra- large dick. Suniya's pussy was warm, wet, and snug, just the way he liked it. She gasped as she felt his manhood smash against her G- spot again. Her breasts bounced and jiggled back and forth as he rocked her with his mighty thrusts.

Holding her around the waist and pulling her into him, he pushed his throbbing dick balls to ass deep with every plunge. The sound of his balls slapping echoed through the large office and bounced off the glass of the panoramic picture windows. Neither of them cared if the sounds of their fucking reached orbiting satellites in deep space. They were too close to a nuclear explosion to care what anyone thought.

Now, Suniya's body was still experiencing spasms from her previous climax. Her pussy clenched, contracted and sucked Mykal's dick as if it was a mouth. He shuddered and moaned, but somehow Mykal held on and managed to control the orgasm that was raging war against him.

Stuffing his hard dick as deep into her as it could go, he plunged on. Another wave of sheer orgasmic bliss snatched the wind from Suniya's mouth and she was slapped onto the shores of Pleasure Island once again.

Her pussy quivered and seized and subsequently choked the damn life out of Mykal's hard, big dick. Overwhelmed with lust he succumbed to the cataclysmic destruction of his release and immediately joined Suniya on that island designed for two.

Mykal stroked harder and faster and seconds later his condom was filled with the fruits of his squirting dick. Still climaxing, Suniya squeezed her pussy muscles around his throbbing cock as he continued to slam in and out of her abyss. Finally drained, he slumped over her back and grabbed the back of the chair for support.

Breathing deeply, he managed to reach around and kiss her face. Suniya turned to him and offered him her lips. Mykal smiled at her as he sampled them.

"I am so glad you dropped by today." He chuckled as he sucked her trembling bottom lip into his mouth. "We'll have to finish this discussion tonight."

Suniya giggled and then ordered. "Silence! No talking!" Mykal chuckled and held her tight.

CHAPTER 20

Victoria woke up at three in the morning from a dead sleep. She sat up on the side of the bed and looked around her lavish master bedroom suite. She looked over at Mykal who had spent the night after their weekly dinner date. He was sleeping soundly.

Suddenly Victoria became dizzy and felt queasy. She bolted across the spacious room to her master bathroom where she vomited in the toilet. She threw up until she was weak. Hugging the toilet she struggled to get herself together.

Washing her face in her marble sink she stared at her image in the large wall mirror. Tears rolled down her face. She had a sinking suspicion what was wrong with her. Cover her face with a wet wash cloth she silently sobbed.

She was happy Mykal remained sound asleep and did not hear her. Stepping into the shower she showered. The warm water calmed her and was instrumental in masquerading her tears.

After brushing her teeth and gargling Victoria felt better, so she returned to bed. She wrapped her body around Mykal's and held him tight. She whispered, "I love you Rome."

She whispered those words not so much that she wanted Mykal to hear them, but because she needed to her herself say them. In the five years that they'd been friends, neither of them once spoke those words out loud. They both somehow feared their relationship would change and come to an abrupt end if they did. Victoria need those words to pierce the atmosphere to legitimize the fact that what she felt was real.

For the remainder of the night she struggled desperately to make sense of what was wrong with her body. Sleep did not return to her. She wrestled all night with the thought that some way, somehow she had become pregnant. She had no clue what she was going to do. The only thing was certain was that Mykal Roman was the father.

CHAPTER 21

Suniya had been running around like a chicken without their head attached for the past month. Her relationship with Mykal was phenomenal, but he required a large portion of her free time. Truth be told, all of her spare time was devoted to him. They hooked up at least three to four times weekly. Long hard days at work were followed by hot sweaty nights of panty dropping, back cracking sex.

No wonder she felt exhausted and run down. She was moody, fatigued and honestly she could use a good nap. The kicker was that all of the late night dinners and rich foods from exotic restaurants has started to take their toll. She'd gain a little weight and wasn't happy about it.

The weight really wasn't a problem, because she wore it well. Her breast were full and inviting and Mykal loved it and the bubble ass that came with it. Her skin had never been smoother, in fact it had an alluring healthy glow. Sure she had to buy some new clothes but it was worth it, because Mykal loved her knew figure.

Naturally, Dani and Jaye immediately noticed. They weren't so sure that the weight gain wasn't as insignificant as Suniya seemed to think. They'd been watching her and she showed all of the signs of something so much more serious. They listened intently as she whined and complained.

"I'm so tired I'm about to faint. I swear I love dating Mykal, but damn, a girl need a break."

"Mr. Mykal Roman would be the one who needed a break if he was my man." Jaye snickered.

"Girl, who you telling! I'd have his ass on life support before I was done with his fine, chocolate ass!" Dani laughed. "I'd be all over his ass like a leotard on the fat lady in the circus. He'd be trying to peel my big ass off of me to get away."

"Yeah that's what you say now." Suniya sighed. "Mykal's a whole lot of man. And he's man with a whole lot of needs. Making love with him is a damn marathon. He'll have your horny ass sucking oxygen directly from the tank in less than an hour."

"Within an hour? Girl, exactly how long does he last?" Dani asked amazed.

"Mykal can go two to three hours on a good night. There's no hit it and quit it with him."

"Cut the bullshit. Suniya! That's not even possible." Jaye laughed.

"Actually, it's not! I read about that Kama Sutra stuff!" Dani chimed in.

"Who said anything about Kama Sutra? No! This is plain old fashioned manly stamina. Each session is a precursor for the next one. I like foreplay like the next woman, but seriously an hour of it! Come on! It was great at first, but now… My nipples are so sensitive I can hard put on a bra. If I wasn't so damn horny I'd run from his big dick ass!"

"Oh my God! Is this little trick complaining about good dick! Really? Really, Suniya! Try not getting any for a couple of years and then you'll really have something to bitch about!" Dani laughed. "Loan him to me for a day, I'll have his ass balled up in the fetal position, sucking his thumb, begging for his binky and a damn nap!"

"Wait a second, Suniya... Your nipples are sensitive and you've gained weight?" Jaye asked surprised as if she just had a revelation.

"Yeah, why?" Suniya asked puzzled by the question.

"Oh hell nah! She's also tired, bitchy and horny!" Dani, immediately picked up on Jaye's train of thought. "Hell to da, hell to the nah!"

"What? What's wrong?" Suniya asked looking back and forth between them.

"Damn it Suniya! Didn't somebody teach you about birth control?" Dani vented.

"Of course I know about birth control! I'm on Depro!" Suniya retorted. "I'm not stupid!"

"Well, apparently you are, because you're pregnant!" Jaye laughed. "Oh my God! How did you let this happen?"

Suniya was in complete shock. It all may sense now. The reality of her situation hit her in the face with the force of a battering. She had allowed herself to get so caught up in Mykal, she forgot to recheck her pregnancy test after their mishap.

Suniya had taken a home pregnancy test a week after the incident. It was negative. Her gynecologist advised her to recheck her pregnancy test within two weeks of her first negative test. Unfortunately, Suniya completely wrapped herself in Mykal and totally forgot, until now.

"Noooo! Oh hell fucking no! That can't be possible! I assured Mykal I wasn't pregnant. How am I going to tell Mykal this two months later? God no! This has to be some kind of virus or the stomach flu or something. Right?"

"Oh it's a stomach flu alright!" Dani laughed.

"Yeah, the kind that goes away in nine months!" Jaye added. "Girl, let me go get you an EPT!"

"It's too late for that! She needs a TDLPT!" Dani laughed.

"What the hell is that?" Suniya asked not getting her humor.

"It's a Too Damn Late Pregnancy Test!" Dani burst into robust laughter and Dani joined her.

"You two bitches are the worse friends ever!" Suniya snickered. "This shit isn't funny! Mykal is going to be pissed! I don't even know how I'm going to tell him."

"I tell you how you're going to tell him. You're going to look him in those big brown eyes of his. Then you're going to open this pretty mouth of yours and say, "I'zsa knocked up Big Daddy! What's we gonna do?" Jaye teased.

"Worst friends ever!" Suniya laughed to keep from crying.

"Tough! We're all you have!" Dani hugged her. "Now let's get this over with."

"Okay." Suniya breathed, scared shitless.

"Don't worry, it'll all work out. He loves you. I can tell" Jaye assured her.

"I hope you're right." Suniya said as she wiped a steady stream of tears from her eyes. "I'm not so sure."

"Are you in love with him?"

"Yes!" Suniya sobbed.

"Good! You know the type of man he is, Suniya. Mykal's honest. He's going to do right by you. He loves you. I can see it in his eyes. Don't cry. Okay?"

"She's right Suniya. Please stop crying before you make me cry. It'll be alright, one way or the other."

Suniya wanted to believe them, but to date Mykal had not declared his love for her. In fact, they were for all practical purposes they were still just casually dating. She knew he liked her a lot, but love was another story.

One thing was certain, Suniya was madly in love with Mykal and she was pretty sure he knew it.

CHAPTER 22

Mykal rolled over at the sound of his phone alarm. Disoriented, he looked around for Suniya. She was up and sitting on the side of the bed trying to get her bearings.

"Morning! How did you sleep?" She asked in a small voice.

"Morning baby. Good. What about you?" Mykal said as he pulled her back into the bed. He was groggy but his nature was wide awake. Pulling her close he sampled her lips.

"Don't even start. Get up! I have a shipment coming in at eight and you have a meeting at seven thirty. So, stop."

"Why should I?" He chuckled as he nibbled seductively on her bottom lip.

"Two words... Morning Breath!" She laughed.

"I wasn't going to say anything, but your breath is a little tart. I'm willing to overlook it just this one time." Mykal teased as he rolled on his back and drug her on top of him.

"Unbelievable." She giggled as she playfully punched him in his shoulder. "You want some ass and you're going to make me do all of the work."

A sexy grin slid quickly across Mykal's handsome unshaved face. "Not really, I figured I'd take over after I convinced you to get things started. You've known me long enough to know that I'm not a lazy lay?"

"Mykal Roman, many people have probably called you many things, but lazy has never been one of them. And I'd never even consider calling you anything except enthusiastic when it comes to sex." She admitted as she leaned in and tasted is soft lips.

Her eyes met his as her hands slid beneath the waist band of his boxer briefs. He was hard and fully erect. It was obvious that he was in need of a little TLC. "I knew I should have dealt with monster last night."

"I tried to warn you." He chuckled as he gazed upon his beautiful woman.

Suniya was an extraordinarily beautiful woman, even with her bed hair, eye cooties and morning breath. She had brown eyes that sparkled like black diamonds. Her long, coal black, natural hair hung mid- way down her back. It was the perfect frame for her stunning face. Her full lips were inviting and Mykal could not resist the urge to kiss them.

Deepening the kiss, he multi tasked by pulling Suniya's tank top over her head. Tossing it on the floor he quickly flipped her on her back. Kissing her softly on her lips he said, "We can do this tonight if you are not up for it. I know you've been tired later."

Suniya powered her way to the top position and straddled his torso. "Don't wimp out now Mr. Roman." Sucking his lips into her moist mouth, she slowly ran her slender fingers through his short cut, wavy black hair. "I'm in love with you. You realize that don't you?"

Mykal dark eyes locked on her. Sampling her lips he considered Suniya's words and just how much he had grown to love her. "Yeah! I'm not sure why you love someone as ugly as me, but I'm just gonna go with it until you come to your senses." He chuckled before kissing her on the forehead.

"Stop playing around. I'm serious." Suniya pouted.

"Who's joking? I'm serious. One day you're going to wake up and take one look at this butt ugly face of mine and run out of here screaming. 'What the hell was I thinking?' Just wait and see!" He teased.

Suniya took a good look at her handsome man. Mykal was a tall glass of chocolate milk. Hard work and clean living had given him a rock hard, lean, sexy body. Speaking of rock hard, Mykal had something else that was always rock hard and ready to go and Suniya loved it. He was an impress package and Suniya felt honored to claim Mykal as her man.

Everything was great between them, except one thing. Suniya was always fatigued and felt run down. She had put off having sex with Mykal the night before because she was physically exhausted. There was no way she'd turn him down again.

Crawling down his body she pulled his boxers down. Mykal grinned as he realized Suniya was officially ready for some love. His manhood popped up strong and proud and Mykal quickly grabbed it to prevent it from punching her in the eye. Suniya slowly discarded the briefs on the side of the bed as she watched him slowly stroke his manhood. Fully erect, Mykal's throbbing dick was an impressive sight.

"Let me take care of that for you Mr. Roman." She smiled as she replaced her small hand with his.

A sexy, devilish smile tugged at the corner of his lips as he watched Suniya firmly stroke his hard nature from base to tip. Her hand was small, but her grip was firm. Mykal's eyes rolled around in his head as her slow methodic hand pleasured him. It had been over a week and a half since Suniya was in the mood for sex, so he knew he was in for a wild ride. Suniya was a lioness in bed.

"Thank you Ms. Simmons." He groaned as Suniya sucked his throbbing dick into the confines of her warm mouth. The sensation was overwhelming, and prompted his hips to gyrate rhythmically against her mouth. "Damn that feels good."

He unconsciously breathed as Suniya hollowed her cheeks and increased the pressure on Mykal's thick dick.

Suniya knew exactly how he liked it. Mykal's eyes rolled back in head and stayed there as Suniya's persistent mouth continued to pleasure him. Her small hands slow stroked his stalk as her moist mouth slid effortlessly back and forth along its length. Mykal was dangerously close to an orgasm, so he grabbed her by her small waist and flipped her on her back in one fluid motion. She was stunned, but pleasantly surprised when he spread her legs and buried his head between her toned thighs.

Suniya gasped as the tip of Mykal's warm tongue licked her clit. "Oh my damn! I missed this!" She hissed as her ass lifted from the bed to bring her pussy flush with his mouth. Mykal grabbed two handfuls of her ass and pulled her even closer as he slurped her love. Suniya responded by grabbing the back of his head and held on tight.

Mykal was like an obsessed man in a pie eating contest. Try as hard as he could, he could not get his feel of her warm, sweet pussy. Sucking her entire shaved mound in his mouth he preceded to devour her one suck and one lick at a time. Soon Suniya exploded into a zillion satisfied microscopic piece.

Grabbing a condom from the nightstand, he quickly strapped up. Mounting Suniya quickly Mykal bumped and humped his way to a very deliciously satisfying orgasm of his own. As the final squirts of his hot cum filled his condom, he kissed her full and deep. Afterwards, they cuddled in each other's arms as they contemplated their bright future.

"I'm pregnant." Suniya quietly announced as she snuggled closer.

"I know." Mykal casually responded and kissed her shoulder blade. "I saw the pregnancy tests when I took out your trash two weeks ago."

"Why didn't you say something?" She asked as she turned to face him.

"And miss this moment? No damn way!" He chuckled.

"You're such an ass! I've been racking my brains for a way to tell you for two weeks and you already knew?" She playfully shoved him.

"Yes I am an ass, but I'm the happiest ass in the world right now!" He assured her before he kissed her tenderly.

Suniya was ecstatic. "We're going to have a baby!" She gleefully squealed as tears burst from her eyes.

"I know." Mykal chuckled. His voice choked with emotion. "I know!"

CHAPTER 23

Suniya was cooking a light meal for dinner. Tonight was her birthday, but she really didn't feel like going out to celebrate. Mykal wanted to take her out for dinner and dancing, but she wasn't up for a crowd. She was tired, her feet were swollen and she just wanted to spend some alone time with her man. As she was chopping vegetables for a garden salad her house phone rang. It was Sissy.

"Happy Birthday to you! You look like a shoe! Happy Birthday dear Boots! And you smell like one too!" Sissy sang loud and off key! "Happy Birthday, Birthday Girl! I can't believe you're turning twenty six today."

Suniya laughed. "I can't believe you call me every year on my birthday and sing that stupid ass song! Thanks Sissy!"

"You're welcome! You know I couldn't forget your Birthday! I'm glad I caught you home."

"Not in much a mood to hang out tonight. So, I decided to stay in and spend some quality time with my man."

"Please don't tell me you've moved another stray into your house. Didn't I tell you to stop feeding strays and they'll go away?"

"FYI, he doesn't live here and he's not a stray. He is…"

"Uh! I don't care! Don't want to hear it and don't really want to get involved in your biz-niz! I was just making a tried and true recommendation. Look, open the garage door. It's raining out here and I don't want to get my hair wet. You know what happens when my hair gets wet."

"Where are you?" Suniya asked stunned.

"Turning down your street as we speak."

"What? Sissy are you serious?" Suniya blurted as she ran to the window to see if she could see Victoria's car. "I don't see you."

"Boots! Just open the garage. I'm pulling in the driveway now."

"Is that you in the black BMW? Did you get a new car?"

"No! I didn't! You did! Now open the damn garage door so I can drop it off!" Victoria giggled.

"Oh my God! You bought that for me?" Suniya screamed, dropped the phone and ran to the garage to meet Sissy.

Sissy pulled into the garage slowly driving a brand new, chromed out, custom enhanced BMW M6 Convertible. Suniya screamed and danced around the garage waiting for her to park and get out.

She was so excited in fact she had completely forgot that she had not told Sissy about her pregnancy. Sissy saw the weight gain immediately and knew she was pregnant. "Fuck!" She breathed beneath her breath. "What ass has she let knock her up?" Refusing to spoil Suniya's Birthday, she pretended not to notice. However, she was thoroughly pissed!

"Happy Birthday baby!" Sissy held out the keys to Suniya's new car.

Suniya was so excited she jumped into Sissy's arm and hugged her tight enough to break her. "Thank you! Thank you! Thank you!" She screamed out.

"You're welcome, just please stop screaming in my damn ear!" Sissy laughed. I saw you looking at the one in parked in front of your store the last time I visited. So, I got you one! Here are your keys, the registration is in the glove compartment and you're ready to go! Just promise me you'll drive safe." Sissy announced as she dangled the keys within Suniya's grasp.

Suniya took the keys, hugged them to her heart and screamed again. Snatching Sissy back into her arms, she covered her face with a hundred tiny kisses. "Thank you Sissy."

Sissy smiled. For a second she thought Suniya was going to call her mom. "You're welcome baby. So do have a few minutes to hangout before your man arrives?"

"Stop! Of course I do. Come on in." Suniya released Sissy and led her into the kitchen.

Sissy trailed behind her and got a good look at just how fat Suniya's ass had grown. "Wow! That's a whale of a tail you've got all of a sudden."

Suniya stopped in her tracks and face Sissy. She suddenly remembered they had not discussed her pregnancy. She nervously turned and faced Sissy. She watched her as she took a seat at the island. Suniya positioned herself across from her. She continued eye Sissy as Sissy eyed her.

Sissy decided that they could fight about it later. After all, it was Suniya's life and her Birthday. "So! What are you cooking?"

"Broiled steak, baked potatoes and a salad." Suniya mumbled as she watched a controlled coolness settle over Sissy. "Sissy we need to talk."

"About what dear? Can I get a bottle of water?"

"Sure!" Suniya went to the refrigerator and returned with a cold bottle of water.

"Thanks!

"I was going to tell you, but I knew you'd be upset."

"Tell me what Boots?"

"Sissy, just stop! I didn't mean for it to happen, it just did!"

Sissy closed her eyes and pondered her words carefully. She was in no position to lecture or chastise Suniya about anything. She'd had her share of mistakes too. Sissy just didn't want this for her daughter.

"Let me ask you a question. Are you happy?" Sissy asked as she armed her bullshit detector and stared Suniya dead in her eyes.

"Yes!" Suniya breathed. "Sissy, I'm in love with him and I think he loves me too!"

"You think he loves you. Is that what you just said?" Sissy shook her head and looked away from Suniya. "Boots, he either loves you or he doesn't, which one is it."

Suniya bit her lips as tears formed in her eyes. Mykal never said it, but she knew in her heart and soul that he was in love with her. "He's in love with me."

"Sissy slowly nodded her head. "Good! Now let me tell you this one thing and we'll never speak of it again."

"Okay." Suniya nodded and spoke in a small defeated voice. Her head dropped and she diverted her eyes from Sissy's glare.

Sissy stood up, reached across the island and cupped Suniya's face in her hands. "Look at me, because I want to be clear when I say this." Tears ran down Suniya's face as she nodded, okay. "If he hurts you or even lays a fingerprint on you or my grandchild, I will have him killed. My uncles will pick him up, beat his ass, drag him away and he will never be seen again. Do you understand?"

"Yes mam!" Suniya sobbed. She was not crying because of the threat. She cried because she finally realized just how much Sissy really loved her.

"Good! Congratulations! I am so very happy for you!" Sissy hugged her tight and kissed her face. Their tears blended on their cheeks as they sobbed. "Oh my God! I'm too young to be a grandma!"

"Suniya giggled. "You're getting old." Suniya pulled a few paper towels from the rack and gave one to Sissy.

Sissy wiped her eyes. "This shit is so crazy. You're going to make a wonderful mom."

"Thank you Mom." Suniya said as she hugged her mother tight. Fresh tears coated their faces.

They finally had a breakthrough in their relationship. Suniya finally allowed herself the luxury of considering Sissy her mom. No words were necessary as the two women held each other and cried. Letting go of all of the craziness and bullshit that divided them they bonded as mother and daughter.

CHAPTER 24

The rain had eased up to a fine drizzle by the time Mykal pulled up in front of Suniya's home. Their relationship had blossomed quickly after the pregnancy and he spent most of his nights there with her. Towards that end Suniya had given him a key.

She'd only been to Mykal's condo a few times and preferred to be home. So, she rarely spent the night there. Still, she felt strange that he didn't offer her a key to his place. Unfortunately, she had used up all of her crazy points and dared make a scene. She figured eventually they move together, so it really didn't even matter.

Mykal entered the house with his key. Suniya was busy in the kitchen making a sour cream and onion topping for the baked potatoes. She welcome Mykal with a tender kiss on the lips as he handed her a beautiful bouquet of flowers.

"Thanks, baby. These are beautiful."

"Not one tenth as beautiful as you are. Happy Birthday, Ms. Simmons." His sexy voice breathed as he deepened the kiss. "I know you said you didn't want to go out, but I certainly didn't expect you to cook. Suniya, I could have cooked."

"Nonsense! It knew you'd be arriving late, so I started dinner. Don't be silly. I love to cook for you."

"Yeah. Sorry, I'm late but I had to pick up your Birthday surprise."

"Don't worry about it. Actually, I'm glad you were running late. Sissy, stopped by and we had a long talk. I told her about the baby and she's excited to meet you."

"Really, Sissy's your big sister right?" Mykal asked as he looked in the refrigerator for a quick snack.

"Yes, I mean no! Never mind, it's a long story. I'll explain it to you later. Anyway, she's freshening up in the bathroom. We kind of had a moment and things got really emotional."

"Oh! She's still here. I didn't see a car." He grabbed and apple and shut the refrigerator door.

"That's because it's in the garage. Follow me and let me show you something."

Mykal followed Suniya to the garage where she showed off her new BMW. He was impressed. They got inside cranked it up and fooled around with the onboard navigation system and a few of the other features.

"Wow! Your sister really went all out for your birthday. I'm luckily to get a birthday card from my sister."

"You never told me you had a sister."

"I have two. It's not like we do a hell of a lot of talking when we're alone together." He grinned as he leaned in for a kiss.

Suniya snickered. "You're right about that." Her lips grew closer to his and Mykal, engaged her in a five alarm whorehouse kiss. They kissed feverishly, almost forgetting they had a guest.

"I hope you know I'm gonna tear that ass up the second your sister leave." He warned her.

"Birthday sex is my favorite gift, so bring your damn A-game." She countered.

"Alright! Just remember, you asked for it." He smiled as they locked the car and returned to the kitchen.

"Oh good, you're out of the bathroom. Sissy, I'd like you to meet Mykal Roman. Mykal, I'd like you to meet the infamous Sissy I've told you little or nothing about."

Mykal's heart leaped into his throat and strangled the hell out of him as his eye fell upon the blonde white woman sitting in at the island. Suniya saw the shock on his face and immediately felt the need to explain.

"Sorry, I forgot to tell you that Sissy was white. I'm biracial."

Honestly, Mykal's brain was racing a thousand meters a second and he didn't hear a damn thing Suniya said. He took a serious long look at the beautiful woman and then blurted, "Tori, what the fuck are you doing here?"

"Me! What the fuck are you doing here! Oh my God! Rome, please do not tell me you fucked my daughter and knocked her up!"

"Your daughter! She said you were her sister!"

"I'm not her damn sister! This is my daughter! How could you do this to me? You fucker!"

"What? Oh I'm the fucker? Ain't this about a fucking bitch! You never told me once you had children. Suniya just turned twenty six! If you're thirty six, that would make you ten when you had her! What kind of bullshit is this?"

The two were so busy arguing that they completely forgot about poor Suniya. She was so shocked by it she almost passed out. Her frail finger clutched the island as she steadied herself. She could not believe it. The man she was in love with had been fucking her mother, sister or whatever the fuck Sissy was to her at any given moment.

Her head pounded as they argued back and forth, shooting accusations and insults to each other as if they were torpedoes. Of all the inappropriate, inconvenient times in the world her baby kicked for the very first time. It was like a call to action for her to check these two crazy idiots.

Screaming at the tip top of her lungs she screamed, "You two nasty mother fuckers have one minute to get the fuck out of my house before I rid the world of both of you!"

'Suniya!" Mykal breathed as he turned to face her.

"Boots! It's not what you think!" Victoria said as she rushed towards Suniya evaded her grasp and ran for her gun.

"Suniya, baby... I can explain!" Mykal called to her as he watched her fish something out of a remote draw in the kitchen.

"Oh can you now? Huh Mykal?" She said as she cocked a bullet in the chamber of the nine millimeter. "I warned you to leave, but you didn't. Now since you and Nasty McNasty over there decided to stay, please explain. Tell me why you were fucking me and fucking my skank ass mother- sister whatever the fuck she think she is to me. Go ahead and explain and I just may let both of you live."

"Suniya Simmons! Put that fucking gun down!" Victoria demanded.

"Fuck you, Sissy! You can't tell me what to do! Since you have so much mouth why don't you explain? How, when and why have you been sleep with my man?"

Mykal looked at Victoria. Both of them threw their hands up in surrender. He nodded for her to tell Suniya what she wanted to know. He could tell by the look in Suniya's eyes that she was fragmented and not herself. She was one flew over the Coo-coo nest and make another fly by.

"Okay baby, just point that gun away. You don't want to shoot anyone by accident. Do you?"

Suniya turned the gun back on Mykal. "You two Mother Fuckas are going to make me shoot both of you if you don't start talking."

"Okay! Okay! I'll tell you." Sissy intervened as they noticed Suniya's gun hand began to tremble and shake. "I met Mykal five years or ago in Miami! We were lovers until he moved to Atlanta. I followed him here to be with him and to be close to you. I had no ideal you two had met, let alone were dating." Victoria spilled in one breath.

"What about you pretty boy? What's your story?" She asked as her eyes narrowed in on Mykal.

"She telling you the truth. I never even knew Victoria had a daughter and had no way of suspecting she had a daughter your age. She told me she was thirty five and I believed her. I told you when I met you I had a friend. Victoria was that friend."

Tears rolled down Suniya's cheeks at an alarming rate as her baby kicked her again. "Do you love her?"

"No! Not the way you speak of. I'm in love with you."

"Whatever!" Suniya snorted. "Funny I had to hold a gun on you to get you to say it! You don't love anyone except yourself, Mykal Roman!"

"Suniya, that's not true and you know! I'm in love with and you can trust me when I say it."

Suniya ignored him and turned her gun and focus on Victoria. "What about you Nasty McNasty? Do you love him?"

Victoria looked at Mykal. He nodded for to go ahead and answer the question. "Yes! I'm sorry, but yes I do!" She squared her shoulders and prepared for the consequences.

"What?" Mykal burst out in shock. "Tori stop playing! This shit isn't a joke! You know we're not in love! Tell her the truth!"

"I just did!" Victoria screamed at him. "You may not love me, but I'm in love with you! And I'm not going to lie to her. I love her too much!"

"Tori! This is insane! You knew I was in love with Suniya! Why are you telling me this bullshit now?"

Because you couldn't see it and you never gave me a chance to say it!" She snapped back.

"Fuck!" Mykal breathed. He just knew Victoria had sealed their fate. He was about to die at the hand of the woman he loved, the mother of his unborn child, over some bullshit. "F-U-C-K!" He screamed loudly. His voice choked with emotions. "This is not my fault! I didn't know! I didn't know! Suniya, I love you! You can kill me if you want but know that I love you! I can prove it!"

"How?"

"Let me get something out of my pocket."

"It better be your damn car keys! Because I've heard enough! I am not going to jail for you two sacks of whorehouse cum! Take Nasty McNasty and get the FUCK OUT!"

Victoria eyes pleaded with Mykal not to say another word. He got the message. He motioned for her to follow his lead and they both backed slowly to the door with their hands raised high. Suniya held the gun on them as they opened the door to leave.

Hurt, Mykal silently cried. Victoria was in shock. "Happy Birthday, Suniya." He said as he slipped his hand in his breast pocket and produced a ring box. He put it on the table by the door and turned and walked out.

CHAPTER 25

Mykal and Victoria got in his car, burned rubber and left. Victoria was hysterical, but Mykal was in no position to console her. He was hurt, confused and shaken at his core. His whole world had just tumbled down and crushed him beneath its weight. One minute he was at Tiffany's purchasing an engagement ring for the mother of his unborn child and the next he was here, fleeing for his life.

Pulling over after they had gone a safe distance, he sobbed loudly. Victoria wrapped her arms around to comfort him and they both cried like two toddlers who missed their mommies. Mykal realized that his lost was great, but Victoria's was greater.

Distraught and unable to drive another mile he called a car to pick them up and a driver to drive his car home. They held each other in silence until the car came. They both were numb, emotionless and pretty much void of life as the climbed in the back of the limo.

It was a thirty minute ride to Victoria's and neither of them spoke a single word until they arrived. Victoria turned to Mykal as she prepared to get out and calmly announced, "I'm pregnant. The baby is yours. I'll talk to you about it later."

Mykal's consciousness was in no position to take another bomb like that. His soul felt like it left his body as the news hit him. It all seemed like a horrific nightmare. Unable to do nothing else, he simply said, "Okay. Call me."

He watched as his driver made sure Victoria got in safe. Once the driver returned and pulled off the effects of the last blow to his heart hit him. Mykal pulled himself up into a ball and cried and cried.

Everything he knew to be real told him that he just lost both of them. The mere thought of that one fact devastated him. He was destroyed. Victoria was his best friend and he'd do almost anything to preserve their friendship. Mykal was in love with Suniya and he'd do any and everything to win her back. His heart told them they were both gone and his soul mourned the lost.

CHAPTER 26

Mykal was on his way to the gym one Saturday morning when Victoria showed up unannounced. As she prepared to ring the bell, he opened the door to leave.

"Hey! I wasn't expecting you? Did I forget a doctor's appointment or something?" He asked confused as she brushed by him into the apartment.

"No! I'm horny! In fact, I'm so horny I could take on the entire Atlanta Braves team and their coaches! I've been masturbating all night and half the morning, but I just can't reach this incredible itch. What the fuck is wrong with me?"

Mykal was stunned. He watched as she headed for his living room and plopped down on the sofa. "Okay... Well, I'm not really sure... But, what do you want me to do about it?"

Victoria looked him and rolled her eyes. "What the hell you think?"

"Oh! Okay! Are you sure?" Victoria rolled her eyes again and just stared at him. "Yeah… Well, if you wait here for me while I hit the gym, I'm pretty sure that I can help you with that problem." He laughed. "Oh my God! You should see your face!"

"Mykal! This shit is not funny! So, I don't know why you're laughing! It's like I'm in heat or some damn nonsense, but nobody wants to fuck me! Look at me! I'm the size of a cow! You did this to me, so you have to take care of this."

Victoria was so frustrated she looked as if she was about to cry. Mykal sat on the couch with her and held her in his arms to console her. Consolation was not what she came for.

"I'm sorry, I shouldn't have laughed that was insensitive. Tori, don't get upset, it's just some hormonal thing brought on by the pregnancy. Look, have some juice and chill here until I get back. I have to make a quick one hour session with my trainer and then we'll work on that itch. I promise I have exactly what you need to scratch it. Okay?"

"Rome, I wish I could wait, but I can't. I need you to handle this right now. If not then I'm just going to the bar and pick up the first horny fuck I see who is willing to fuck me." She pouted as she unconsciously rubbed and squeezed her nipples through her clingy royal blue dress.

"Tori, it can't be that bad. Just let me hit the gym real quick. Alright?"

Victoria did not respond in words. She tore away from his arms and walked across the room. She stopped ten or so feet away from him and stood there as if she was about to give a speech. She had a nasty wiggle to her walk. The rhythm of her ass quickly got Mykal's attention. She smiled as she felt his eyes on her firm ass. Victoria was horny and lust was gnawing at her pussy. She was determined to get some dick.

Sticking her index finger in her mouth she eyed him to make sure she had his full attention. Mykal's dick was rising to attention. So yes, she had his undivided attention. Victoria smiled as she seductively removed her form fitting dress and tossed it to the floor.

Mykal scooted forward in the chair to watch her performance. He was officially all in now. His dick grew harder and larger by the millisecond. Whatever Victoria was up to he wished she'd hurry up. The gym could wait, he wanted to fuck.

Victoria was wearing only a black lace thong beneath her dress. Mykal unconsciously licked his lips as he lustfully surveyed her fineness. He smiled as he acknowledged his approval and the fact that she was an exceptional beauty.

Victoria smiled and winked at him as she slowly ran her hands over her chiseled body. They roamed over her flat sculptured abs towards the waistband of her thong. She paused briefly before her fingers slipped beneath her panties and into her pussy.

Intrigued Mykal watched as her hands moved beneath the fabric of her lace thong. Victoria toyed with her pussy, and stroked it as if it was a kitten. His eyes darkened with lust as he watched her pleasure herself.

Her fingers rubbed and rolled around her clit. Her hips rolled and gyrated against her busy hand as pleasure and lust coursed through her. Victoria closed her eyes tight and licked her lips as she continued to finger herself for her pleasure and Mykal's amusement.

He watched intently as she writhed uninhibitedly against her hand as her needed swell greater. Pulling her thong completely off Victoria fondled and fingered her hot pussy, occasional licking her own juices. Intoxicated with lust she squeezed her breast hard with one hand and savagely finger fucked herself with the other.

Spreading her slit apart, to show the pink inner folds of her wet cunt, Victoria plunged two finger in and out her dripping pussy. Fingering herself madly she thrust her hips back and forth to crazed rhythm which only she could hear.

Mykal had officially seen enough. Victoria was a few strokes short of insanity or a breath snatching orgasm. He didn't know which, but he wanted to be balls deep when it occurred. His pants was open and he was slow stroking a monstrous erection. He motioned her to him and Victoria moved slowly towards him as she licked her juices from her wet fingers.

Kneeling at his feet like a cat, Victoria reached for his hard dick. Grabbing it, she sucked feverishly on it as if it contained water from the fountain of youth. With the palms of her hands she rolled the loose skin covering his rigid cock back and forward as she sucked him off.

Victoria loved to suck Mykal's dick. It tasted delicious. She lived for him to shoot his hot creamy load in her throat. She enjoy it immensely. She loved it almost as Mykal loved seeing her swallow his cum.

Today however, Victoria had an irritating itch in her pussy that desperately needed to be scratched. All she could think about was Mykal slamming his fat, long dick balls deep into her greedy pussy. She wanted him to split her wide open with that torpedo he called a dick.

Luckily, they were on the same page, because that was exactly what Mykal planned to do! "Let me get a condom from my gym bag so I can fuck you." He groaned as her mouth brought him dangerously closed to squirting his seed in her mouth.

"I have one in my purse. Get it out." She replied as she briefly popped his throbbing dick of her mouth.

Mykal did not argue. Normally he'd rather stick his hand in a garbage disposal than in a woman's bag. Victoria was carrying a small clutch, so he grabbed it from the end table beside and retrieved the condom. He opened it and prepared to strap up.

"Give it to me." Victoria breathed around his dick.

Mykal gave her the pink condom and watched in amazement as she used her mouth to roll it onto his big dick. "Woman you are incredible." He breathed. "Come on, it time for a ride."

Victoria climbed into his lap and straddled his enormous dick. She sampled his lips and stared deep into his eyes as the mushroom head of his dick slid into her tight slit. She looked at him, and saw lust and excitement dance in his eyes as she slowly rocked back and forth on his hard.

Beyond aroused, Victoria fought the urge climax as Mykal grabbed her by her thin waist and humped upward to meet her downward stroke. Instantly, their body's moved in perfect harmony.

Victoria was in dick paradise, and she knew it. Her pussy was dripping juice down the inside of her thighs as Mykal filled her pussy from wall to wall with his enormous cock.

"Fuck me! That's it fuck me with that big black dick! Come on and fuck me! I'm almost there! Ah shit that's it! Fuck me!" She hissed in his face like a crazed animal.

Mykal's entire dick was in her now. He fucked up into with the force of ten men. His strong hands grasped her ass and pulled her onto hard, which slammed his extra-large cock even further into her. Victoria fucked back with equal fury.

She could feel the base of his dick as it rubbed against her clit. Her itch was so close yet seemed so far away. The grinding pressure from it brought on a swarm of pleasure and a thunderous orgasm. Her pussy thumped violent and contracted around his Mykal's.

He recognized tell- tale signs of her orgasm. Victoria's body thrashed wildly and she thrust against him as if shit was attempting to stab a whole in her gut with Mykal's steel rod. Suddenly, Victoria opened her mouth to screech, but had lost the ability to scream or make a single noise. Her mouth was open but no sounds escaped. She appeared to be squawking like a baby bird with laryngitis begging for food.

Mykal could feel the super strong spasms from her climax deep within her quivering pussy. He knew she was battling a beastly demon of a climax. Her tremors were so forceful they felt as if they were milking his dick. His hips slammed upward as he snatched her hips downward as hard as he could. He was determined to stuff his dick into her until he came out of her mouth.

Overwhelmed with need as well, Mykal's orgasm crashed over him immediately after hers and he was helpless to stop it. "Ah Fuck! I'm coming! Fuck me back! I'm coming! Fuck this hard black dick! Fuck it!" He snarled, hissed and growled.

Somehow, Victoria heard him and obeyed. Grinding, gyrating, grunting and gasping for air the two lovers fucked hard and furious until their tsunami of pleasure finally subsided and rendered them useless.

Victoria smothered his mouth with a sloppy wet kiss before sucking and biting into the flesh of his neck. Mykal quickly pushed her off of him and stood up. She landed on her ass dazed and confused. She smiled deviously as she watched him undress at the speed of sound.

"Stand up!" His hoarse voice ordered. Victoria immediately complied without saying one word. Turn around and bend over and grab your ankles!" Mykal commanded as he methodically slow stroked his still hard dick and then sheathed it with another condom from Victoria's purse. She whimpered with anticipation as she bent over at the waist, spreading her toned, tanned ass before him.

"I can't! I can barely see my ankles, let alone grab them." She whined. Victoria struggled to bend but her round belly kept getting in the way.

"Don't worry, that's far enough." Mykal groaned as he positioned himself behind her.

Placing two fingers in her pussy he slowly finger fucked her. She instantly responded by covering his fingers with her juices. Mykal removed those fingers and rubbed his fully erect dick along her wet slit. Victoria groaned as he slid it into her wet pussy ad swirled it around.

Pulling out abruptly he lifted her ass up higher and rubbed his wet dick along her long crack until it reached her asshole. Pressing firmly he introduced the large mushroom head of his dick into the tight orifice.

"Yes! Yes! Fucking hell yes! Fuck my ass Mykal! Fuck me hard in my ass!"

Mykal's eyes rolled around in his head as he inched his Lochness monster inch by inch into the tight virgin ass. He knew how to get to her itch and he was determined to scratch the hell out of it. Until now, Victoria had never offered him her asshole.

This was an opportunity of a lifetime and Mykal was going to take full advantage of it. A menacing grin transformed his handsome features as his dick bottomed out in Victoria's rectum. Swiveling his hips and swirling his dick inside her he stretched her to get a perfect fit. Then he fucked into her tight anus with one mission... To satisfy her oversexed, can't get enough, dick loving ass once and for all!

Needless to say, Mykal never made it to the gym that day. Victoria made sure he got a good workout at home. Three rounds later they moved to his bedroom.

CHAPTER 27

Understandably, Suniya immediately isolated herself from Mykal and Victoria. She refused to take either of their calls. They both agreed to give her some space and allow her to make the first move.

Two weeks passed and she slipped into the depths of depression. The thought of Victoria screwing Mykal sickened her. The concept that her mother was in love with her man maddened her. Still, she couldn't get their twisted situation off of her mind. Worse yet, she still loved them both and missed them tremendously, which repulsed her even more.

Sick and tired of being sick and tired she decided to reach out to Victoria. She was her blood, like it or not and Suniya knew that eventually she'd have to forgive her. Mykal could be replaced, but Victoria was all she had.

Suniya never knew her dad's side of the family and her grandmother was dead. Victoria was her only family short of distant cousins and two great uncles. Suniya wanted her child to have a family connection and Victoria was the only real family she had left. Besides, she had to get answers. So, Suniya made up a lame excuse to call her.

Victoria was home in the bed, beneath the covers, with the drapes closed tightly when her phone rang. Like Suniya and Mykal for that matter, she had slipped into a dark melancholy. The ring tone was familiar and she instantly identified the caller as Suniya.

Diving for the phone and answering it at the very last ring she said, "Boots, thank God it's you. I thought I'd never hear from you again. I called and called, but you wouldn't answer my call. I was worried sick. Honey, how have you been doing?"

Suniya said not a word as Victoria rambled on and on. The sound of her voice instantly brought tears to her eyes. She wanted to hang up and crawl into bed and cry herself to asleep. Her emotions were all over the place. She was angry. She was mad. She was hurt and she needed a hug from her mother.

Choking down the lump of feelings which had formed in her throat she somehow managed to speak. "Hi Sissy."

Victoria heard the pain in her daughter's voice and instantly began to wipe the flood of tears that poured down her face like rain. "Boots please don't cry. I can't stand for you to cry. Please stop."

"I wish it was that easy. In case you don't know, I lost everything I loved on my birthday, of all days and I haven't stopped crying since."

"Boots, you didn't lose Rome and you certainly didn't lose me. Rome is in love with you."

"Stop right there. I didn't call to talk to you about Mykal Roman. I called to talk to you about us. Sissy, I don't have anyone in this world but you. Somehow, someday, someway we'll get passed this, but Mykal and I are finished. So, I'd appreciate if you never bring his name up in my presence again. What happened between the three of us was straight nasty and I do not want to be reminded of it ever again. Okay?"

"I understand. I'm sorry I brought his name up."

"Sissy, I was wondering if you'd meet me for lunch. I don't want to bring my child into this world without family. I realize that you do not like to talk about my dad, but now more than ever I feel it's important that I get to know that side of my family. I figured we could discuss this over lunch and start to repair the rift in our relationship. I'm sure you agree, the sooner we start mending this fence the better."

Victoria was silent. She knew exactly how Suniya felt about Mykal, because he told her. Suniya never wanted to see Mykal again. She made it plainly clear that she wanted him out of her life. The fact that they were having a baby made that near impossible, but Suniya was determined to cut him off like a gangrenous limb.

Naturally, Victoria's heart leaped at the opportunity to see her daughter and make amends. The problem was that Victoria was also carrying Mykal's child and Suniya didn't know. Victoria didn't tell Suniya about her pregnancy for fear she'd suffer the same fate.

So, Victoria decided to keep her pregnancy a secret from her daughter. She knew Suniya was too fragile to handle it.

Initially, she considered aborting her baby, but Mykal begged her not to terminate her pregnancy. She was shocked to discover that Mykal was willing to raise the baby as a single dad. So, she agreed to carry the child to term and relinquish custody and all paternal rights to Mykal the day the baby was born.

Hiding the fact that she was pregnant seemed like a sound plan at the time, but now Victoria realized her plan was flawed. Suniya would be devastated the moment she realized Victoria was pregnant. Their fragile relationship would take its final blow and she'd lose her daughter forever. Victoria was trapped and she knew it. Her only move was to confess.

"Sissy, are you still there. I know this is difficult for you, but I feel it's a starting point for us to reveal. All you'll have to do is give me his name and I'll do the rest. You'll never have to be involved with him or his family, unless you want to. Okay?"

"Boots there's something I need to tell you first. I thought I could keep it from you until we were on stable ground, but I can't. You need to know and I don't want it to blind side you. I'd love to have lunch with you, but I need to tell you this first."

"What is it Sissy? And please tell me the truth this time." Suniya asked. She was one hundred per cent certain that Victoria was going to cop out by saying her father was dead. Victoria hesitated. "Come out with it Sissy. Our reconciliation will never work unless you find a way to be honest and frank with me. I am not a child, so please stop treating me like I'm one."

Victoria counted to three and then she blurted, "I'm pregnant and Rome's the father."

Suniya was silent. She assumed her mind was playing tricks on her so she asked for confirmation of what she just heard. "Say that again. I didn't hear you."

"Boots, I'm pregnant by Rome." Victoria sighed. "I'm sorry. I didn't know how to tell you until now."

Suniya dropped the phone as an invisible force stopped her heart and choked the life out of her. The remainder of everything she held dear and loved instantly vanished. Victoria was what remained of her world and now in the blink of an eye she'd lost her.

"No! No! No! Nooooooo!" Suniya screamed at the top of her lungs. That's not true!"

"Boots! Please! It happened before you even met him! I wanted to terminate the pregnancy, but he begged me not to. You have to believe me!" The emotionally distraught Victoria pleaded. Suniya became silent, but Victoria could hear the faint sounds of a wounded sob in the distance. Victoria clung to the phone and sobbed with her.

The two women cried over the phone for what seemed like an eternity and a day before Suniya picked up the phone to speak. "Congratulations." Suniya calmly breathed and then hung up.

CHAPTER 28

Late one night around one o'clock in the morning Mykal's doorbell rang. To his absolute surprise it was Suniya. It both startled and frightened him. He hadn't spoken to her in over three months.

He wrestled with opening the door or pretending he wasn't home. She was furious when she found out Victoria was pregnant by him. They had a big fight and she vowed to never speak to him again.

It was late and he didn't want to fight. Suniya was persistent and rang the bell again and again. It was obvious she was not going to leave without seeing him. After closer inspection of her demeanor, on his monitor, Mykal realized she wasn't angry. Actually, she looked worn and run down. So, he opened the door, determining she just wanted to talk.

Suniya walked in and headed straight for the bedroom. "Come on let's get this over with so I can go to sleep."

Mykal stared at her confused. "Get what over with?"

"Seriously Mykal? I'm pregnant, the size of a baby elephant, I can't see my damn feet and my koochie won't stop thumping. What? Do you think I drove all the way over here to get you to fix me a damn peanut butter and jelly sandwich?" She sarcastically asked. "Get undressed. I'll meet you in the bedroom I have to pee."

Mykal stood in the middle of his living floor with his mouth hung open. "What the fuck?" He breathed beneath his breath.

Suniya's cunt ached for the giant hard dick which proudly hung between Mykal's muscular thighs. The fire between her legs caused her head to swim as it slowly built into a raging inferno which would not allow her to rest at night. Tonight, she was determined there would be satisfaction for that insatiable burn. Mykal's warm, thick cock would scratch that itch her vibrator could not reach or relieve, she confidently assured herself.

"Hurry up! I'm tired. I haven't slept soundly in weeks. I have to get to bed." She called out from the guest bathroom.

When Suniya finally entered the bedroom Mykal was waiting for her. He was nude just as she ordered.

"Suniya I..."

"Sh! No talking. I don't want to hear it unless it's dirty talk. We are not back together and we're not getting back together. This is simply a fuck! Okay?"

Naturally, that wasn't what Mykal wanted, but he was willing to take whatever ground Suniya relinquished. He knew it wouldn't be easy to win her back, but he was willing to do anything to try, even this.

"Okay." He simply responded. "Sex only!"

"You knocked me up, so it's your responsibility to fuck me when nobody else will!"

"I understand." He simply agreed.

Mykal's hand began to slowly slide back and forth along the length of his big dick. He knew Suniya was undoubtedly horny and he'd have to put in work to satisfy her.

Suniya watched the object of her desire double in size before her eyes. Lifting her eyes from Mykal's monstrous manhood to meet his, Suniya ordered, "Lie down in the center of the bed on your back."

A warm, accommodating smile curled the corners of his mouth. "Anything you say. I'm at your service for the rest of the night." Mykal said as lay in the center of the king size bed, flat on his back.

Suniya quickly engineered her legs to position her pregnant frame so she was straddling his face and carefully lowered her quivering pussy onto his warm mouth. She paused to wait for the heat of his eager mouth to sweep over her hungry pussy. Mykal's hot, wet tongue slithered a path along the slit of her soft, moist, lips, Suniya shivered with pleasure.

"Oh my God, yes!" She unconsciously groaned.

The thick tongue on her sensitive pussy instantly drove Suniya to the brink of insanity. Licking her lips she tried to concentrate on the pleasure, Mykal's mouth was giving her cunt. She rubbed her sore nipples and squeezed her sensitive breast as he continued to tease and lick her wet slit with the tip of his tongue.

Suniya's thick thighs held his head locked in a vise grip, holding it right in place. His face was engulfed with the smell and taste of her horny pussy. He was her captive and she wasn't going to release him until he pleased her.

Suniya quickly found herself gyrating on his mouth. Her hips rolled and tumbled to the motion and rhythm of his tongue. Each movement designed to build up to an orgasm that would rock her body with a convulsive, earthshattering climax.

She was so in tuned to her own pleasure she did not realize that her bulky pregnant frame was smothering poor Mykal. He was breathing heavy and unable to successfully catch his wind. He tried desperately to lift her up but her ass was too heavy and Suniya was not offering any assistance.

Slapping the side of her ass trying to get her attention, he exhaled and tried to gulp air from her juicy pussy. Suniya felt his mouth suck and blow into shouldering hot grotto and she loved the sensation. It only prompted her to rub her wet cunt harder onto his mouth.

Fearful of smothering to death in her wet pussy, Mykal screamed her name with a long muffled growl into her cunt. It echoed and vibrated on the walls of her vagina and captured Suniya's undivided attention. She giggled realizing she had almost smother the pour man to death.

Climbing off of him she reclined on her back and waited for him to continue eating her greedy pussy. Mykal rolled his eyes at her, but he knew better than to say anything. Besides, he wanted this as bad as she did. He just didn't want to smother to death to get it.

Crawling between her open legs, his thick, wet tongue went back to licking the folds of her sensitive pussy. Suniya's head was swimming in an ocean of desire as Mykal drank from the fountain of her soaking wet walls. He licked and sucked and licked until there was nothing left to drink.

"Yes! That's it, please don't stop." She groaned and moaned as she tore at her heavy swollen breasts.

Suddenly, she felt the tug of his mouth on her swollen clit as Mykal sampled it. Enjoying its taste he sucked deep into the depths of his mouth. Suniya yelped and then there was a breathtaking pause. The next thing either of them knew she was battling a breath snatching, leg numbing, knees buckling orgasm.

Mykal showed her absolutely no mercy. His tongue immediately darted in and out of her steaming hot pussy as it flooded with her orgasmic juices. Her pussy walls trembled and shook from the aftershock of her tidal wave of pleasure.

Her head was foggy from her raging orgasm. She could hardly think. The sensation of Mykal's tongue snaking in and out of her pussy was overwhelming. She felt a second climax swell within her belly. Her orgasm gushed its nectar onto his tongue and he lapped it up like sweet cream. His tongue danced wildly inside of her pushing her towards the edge of annihilation.

Returning to her clit, Mykal gnaw and tugged and pulled on it as it was a tasty gumdrop. He was determined to make her climax again. The sensation overpowered her and Suniya immediately erupted into her second release. That's when Mykal heard his cue.

"Fuck me! Fuck me hard!"

Bouncing to his knees in a split second, he wishboned her thighs, aimed his throbbing hard dick at her wet entrance and rammed his cock into her balls to ass deep. Holding her legs open Mykal went to work on the ache in Suniya's pussy that wouldn't allow her to sleep at night.

"Yes... Yes... Yes... That's it!" She seemed sang as he hammered into and punched her G-spot in the mouth, repeatedly.

"Does that feel good? Huh? Is that the spot? Ah fuck yeah! That's the spot! Come on baby... Fuck me back!" He hissed as his granite hard dick plunged ass to balls deep into center of Suniya's heat.

"Humping her hips at him she struggled to get every delicious inch of that cock inside her eager horny, greedy pussy.

"Ah shit! Yes! That's it! Don't stop! Fuck faster! Fuck harder!" Suniya screamed, feeling Mykal's monstrous manhood smash against the walls of her mashing against the walls of her Quivering pussy.

Mykal's climax was closing in. His growls, grunts and groans pierced her ears and fueled her need. The soft whimpers of a wounded animal who needed to be put out of their misery escaped her throat. Moments later orgasm number three slapped her across her face giving her the release she sought and her body craved.

Just when she thought she'd die, Mykal shout his hot load and revived her with its warmth. His hard shaft hosed her sensitive pussy with its soothing balm, filling her womanhood to capacity and satisfying her primal urges.

Mykal's orgasm drained him. He climbed from between her thighs and collapsed on his back. The exhausted Suniya rolled towards him, wrapped herself in his strong arms and quickly fell asleep.

The next morning when Mykal woke up she was gone without a trace. If he didn't know better he would have believed it never happened. She didn't return his calls or texts. She'd gotten what she came for and she was finished with him.

Little did Mykal know that Suniya really wanted to stay with him forever, but circumstances dictated that she had to let him go. The anxiety and stress that their sick love triangle had subjected her to was too much for her. I put too much strain on the baby and too on her heart. She had no other choice, but to leave him alone.

CHAPTER 29

Two month passed since Victoria announced to Suniya that she was pregnant. The news of Victoria's pregnancy was more than Suniya could handle. For the sake of her sanity, Suniya rescinded the olive branch and went back into isolation.

She refused to take calls from either Mykal or Victoria. Mykal was going mad without her, but there was nothing he could do. He knew Suniya still loved him, so he agreed to give her space and time to work out her issues. Determined to move beyond their past and rebuild her relationship with her mother, Suniya made a surprise visit to Victoria's home.

Sissy literally sprinted to her front door, when Suniya called and said she was at the door. Excited, she flung it open and her very pregnant daughter was standing there clutching a picnic basket of food. Her knuckles had turned white from holding the handle so tight. Suniya held on to that basket as if it was the very last piece of her sanity. Victoria tried to take it from her, but she wouldn't let it go until they were inside.

Once inside Victoria led her through the contemporary mansion towards the great room. Tears leaked from Suniya's eyes as they fell on her mother's pregnant belly. Victoria was all belly and breasts. She had a yellow sweat suit on and resembled big bird.

Somehow the thought prompted Suniya to snicker. Soon her snickered turned into a chuckled and morphed into a robust laugh. "Oh my God! Sissy, you look like Big Bird!"

"Who? I know Barney did not just call me Big Bird!" Victoria laughed with her. "Oh my God! You're right! I do look like Big Bird!" Victoria laughed as she caught her reflection in the large antique mirror in the foyer. "I didn't realize a person's ass could quadruple in size in a matter of months. Yet, look at my kadunkadunk!"

"Yeah! Report that fact to my ass. The post office called me and told me they had given my ass its very own zip code!" Suniya joined her at the mirror to compare ass size."

"Yeah, but at least yours is round and cute. If you didn't have that belly you could be considered a big booty cutie. Me, however... My ass is shaped like a damn cereal box, flat and wide. I actually look more like Sponge Bob then Big Bird."

"You're right, you do. I was just trying to be nice!" Suniya laughed.

"Oh Boots! I missed you so much!" Victoria responded as she grabbed her daughters in her arms and hugged her tight. "I thought I'd never see you again and here we are laughing about our flabby asses."

"Hey! Speak for yourself... I got a little cellulite, but you can bounce a stone off my ass it's so tight." Suniya giggled. "Sissy, I missed you too and I missed us! I was just kidding around, you look great!"

Victoria affectionately rubbed her belly as her baby changed positions in her womb. "Thanks for saying that Boots."

Suniya saw the baby move and reached out to touch the spot. "What are you having a girl or a boy?"

"Actually, I don't know. We decided we didn't want to know." Victoria instantly noticed the wrinkle in Suniya's brow when she said the word, we. "Boots I wish I could go back in a time machine and change everything that happened. If I could I'd go back five years ago to the night I met Rome and I would go home alone that night. If I could do it I would. You know that right?"

"Let's not talk about it. Oddly, I don't have any more energy to devote to this situation. It's clear that fate has decided to fuck all three of us up the ass without a condom. So, I refuse to let it ruin my life. I'm healthy and I have a baby who will need a mother who's sane. So, as far as I'm concerned, it is what it is. I'm done beating myself up and obsessing over it."

"What about Rome?" Victoria asked stunned by Suniya's cavalier attitude about their circumstances.

"Who Mykal? What about him?"

"So, does this forgive and forget attitude extend to him?"

Suniya sighed deeply after considering Victoria's question. "I understand he was a victim of fate just like we were. There's no malice between us. I just don't think it's a healthy relationship to pursue, especially in light of the fact that we're having ghetto twins."

"You're carrying twins?" Victoria sked confused.

"No, you and I are having what they call ghetto twins. It's when two women have babies by the same man at around the same time."

"That's nasty." Victoria blurted without thinking.

"Yeah! Now multiply it times one hundred and you have our situation, nasty to the nth power. Your child is my brother and argumentatively my nephew. Sissy, I can't carry this... Hell, I can't even process it. When you told me a few minutes ago I almost lost my mind, until my baby moved to bring me back to reality. She needs me and I need her. To be honest with you, I really don't want to have to explain to her that her brother is also her uncle and perhaps her cousin."

"Look, that's not going to happen. And for the record, like it or not or believe it or not, Boots I am your birth mother."

Suniya sighed deeply. "Okay if that's true I need to know about my father and his family."

Victoria studied her daughter. She had hoped to keep the identity of Suniya's father and the circumstances a secret from her. Now, she realized that honesty was the only bridge she had left to maintain a connection with her daughter. Suniya was right. She wasn't a child and she deserved to know.

"Let's have lunch first. Then I'll tell you everything."

"That sounds good. I'm starving."

Victoria and Suniya sat down to eat. Suniya had made a picnic basket full of their comfort foods. She packed peanut butter and jelly sandwiches, tomato soup and cupcakes and gummy bears for desert. When she was a child Victoria would often take her to the park and they'd have a picnic with the exact same things.

Victoria's eyes welled with tears the moment she saw the meal Suniya had prepared. She knew instantly that it was a peace offering. Victoria realized more than ever it was time to tell Suniya the truth. As they cleaned up their mess Victoria began the tale slowly.

"I was thirteen when he moved in with us. They were engaged, well so my mother informed me. He seemed nice enough at first. As time went on he lost his job and started drinking. Mom was a nurse as you know. She started taking extra ships at night to pay the mortgage and the bills. That's when it started."

"Oh Sissy know!" Suniya breathed horrified by what she was hearing.

"I fought him off as best I could. Some nights I'd go to bed with six layers of clothes. He was usually drunk and would get frustrated at trying to get me. Then one night he drugged my soda. I don't know what he used but it knocked me out. All I know is I woke up naked, covered with cum... Every orifice of my body was sore. Two months later I realized I was pregnant with you."

Victoria recited the story as if she was Zombie. Her face was emotionless. Her body was upright and stiff. Her voice was monotone. She was telling the story to an invisible being. She never once looked at Suniya.

Suniya was horrified. She had no clue the man she knew as her grandmother's husband was in fact her father. Actually, she never met him. He died before she was born in some kind of freak Everglade boating accident. A former insurance agent, he was heavily insured. He insurance claims paid out to the sum of two million dollars.

Suniya wept silently as Victoria continued. "After my mom found I was pregnant she confronted me about the father, but I was afraid to name him. I finally confessed to Uncle Billy what had happened out of fear he'd try to rape me again. Three days later he was dead. Uncle Billy apparently told Uncle Bobby and they took care of him. I don't know what actually happened. All I know is no one ever mentioned the father of my baby again."

"Oh, Sissy I didn't know. I'm so sorry that happened to you. How can you even look at me?" Suniya sobbed as she flung herself around Victoria and sobbed like a baby.

"Because I love you. I love you so much Boots I'd give up my life so you could live for another day. This stuff with you, me and Rome is killing me. I can't lose you over it. You're all I have."

"But Sissy what he did to you was so vial and disgusting. Oh God I didn't know I'm so sorry! I'm so sorry!" She cried. "Sissy, I'm so sorry!"

Victoria grabbed Suniya by the face and looked her dead in her eyes. "You have nothing to be sorry for. You are the best thing I've ever done. You are the most beautiful thing I've ever known. Yes! What happened to me was ugly, but it brought me you. So don't ever be sorry about what happened to me, because I'd relive it a hundred times just to have you in my life." She declared through her tears. Clutching Suniya close they cried together.

From that second on Suniya knew three things with certainty. One, Victoria was her mother. Two, Victoria loved her truly, fully and unconditionally. Three, any and all animosity she had towards her was casted into the sea of forgetfulness, never to be brought up again.

They both agreed that day to move on. The mother and daughter vowed to put anything and everything that threatened to separate them behind them, including their love for Mykal Roman.

CHAPTER 30

Six Months Later...

Time passed quickly and old wounds slowly healed. Victoria had a handsome baby boy and signed over full custody to Mykal, as they had agreed, the day he was born. He named the baby Mykal Roman, Jr., no surprise there.

Victoria's relationship with Suniya was very delicate to say the least. She realized sticking around, raising a child with Mykal was not conductive to reconciliation with her daughter. So, Victoria decided to place some time and distance between them. After the baby was born she returned to her home in Miami and to her ex-husband, Richard Dickerson.

Although she left the marriage abruptly, they parted as friends. Victoria contacted Tricky Dick and took him up on his offer to have a child for him. She had mastered pregnancy and had the stretch marks and flabby gut and ass to prove it. So, she figured she'd might as well take advantage of her situation.

They were remarried in a quaint ceremony at Tricky Dick's new mansion in the presence of his family and close friends. Victoria was artificially inseminated three days later, after the sum of twenty million dollars was deposited into her personal bank account.

Naturally his mother was pissed, but she soon got over it once you discovered Victoria was carrying her first grandbaby. After all of those years Catherine Dickerson finally found a reason to like her daughter in-law. By some miracle, Victoria even managed to tolerate her just a little bit more.

~*~*~

Suniya gave birth to a beautiful little girl who surprisingly looked just like Suniya's mother, Victoria. Suniya named her daughter, Makayla Roman. Life was challenging as a single mom, but Makayla's dad was always willing to pitch in and keep Makayla whenever necessary. Mykal was a model father. He hired a full time nanny to help Suniya care for her. He also established a healthy trust fund for Suniya to provide for his daughter in lieu of monthly child support payments.

As for Mykal, he quickly settled in to the life of a single dad. He moved into Victoria's four bedroom house and hired a live in Nanny to care for his son. He had complete custody of Mykal, Jr. and enjoyed joint custody of Makayla. She spent the weekend at his home every other week.

His business continued to thrive and grow by leaps and bounds. Mykal had become a very rich and successful man. Unfortunately, his success was not as sweet as he expected or dreamed it would be.

Mykal moved to Atlanta to start a business, find a wife and have some children. Fate had dealt him a very shitty hand from Mykal's point of view. Just when he was about to have it all, destiny snatched away the one thing he could not live without, Suniya.

Mykal was hopelessly in love with her, but Suniya could not get past the fact that he had a child by her birth mother. Understandably it was a bitter pill to swallow. He prayed with time that by some miracle she'd find a way to choke that nasty pill down and allow him to unite his family.

Mykal got sick to his stomach and teary eyed every time he had to take his daughter home. He wanted the four of them to live together as a family. He knew Suniya was still in love with him. He could see it in her eyes. Still, they were no closer today to reconciliation than they were the day they broke up.

Oddly enough, Mykal refused to take another lover. His son, his business and his right hand sustained him. He wanted to be ready when Suniya returned and he didn't want anything or anyone to stand in his way. So, he remained celibate in hopes that love would prevail all of the bullshit they had gone through.

It was a nice summer day when he pulled into Stone Mountain Park. He rode around looking for Makayla's nanny's car but didn't see her. She was supposed to meet him with Makayla. Parking in his usual spot he waited for her.

Then a miracle happened. Suniya pulled up beside his SUV. His dick changed position the second it heard her sweet voice. He couldn't believe she was there.

"Hey Mr. Roman. I've been riding around here looking for you for twenty minutes. This is a big place." She smiled as she spoke through the car window. "Do you need her stroller?"

"No! I have one… I have a big stroller… One for both of them." He nervously stumbled over his words. Mykal was so excited to see Suniya he could hardly speak without getting tongue tied.

Suniya giggled. She recognized his nervous and was flattered that she still had that kind of effect on him. "Okay, should we get out now? This is my first time here, so you'll have to walk me through this."

"Are you walking with us?" He asked stunned.

"Sure! Why not?" She smiled as she engaged his eyes for approval. "It's a beautiful day and I'm off. So, I might as well enjoy it in the park with you guys."

Mykal tried to mask his excitement and casually replied, "Great! I could use some adult contact."

Suniya started laugh. "Really, because I thought if anybody was getting any, Mykal Roman would definitely be getting his share." She teased.

Mykal smiled, then looked away embarrassed. It was just the tension breaker they needed to dispel all of the nervous tension that had formed between them. "You know that's not what I meant, right?"

"Well, maybe not, but it's what you said." Suniya giggled. "Let me grab Makayla and I'll be right over."

Mykal's heart raced. Something was different about Suniya today. She was blatantly flirting with him. He hadn't seen her this happy and relaxed since her birthday before the fight.

Filled with new found hope, he rushed to get out of the truck. Mykal, Jr. was napping in the car seat. So, Mykal let him sleep a little longer while he got the double stroller from his trunk. He had just finished getting it ready when Suniya appeared with his daughter.

"Ah! Here's my pretty girl." He cooed and kissed his daughter as he took her from Suniya's arms. "Daddy missed you. Did you miss daddy?"

"Do you want me to get Mykal, Jr.?" Suniya asked, as Mykal, doted on his daughter.

Mykal was stunned. Suniya rarely mentioned his son's name, let alone offer to hold him. This was a big milestone, a turning point in their healing process and he knew. All he had to do was to find a way not to fuck it up!

"Yeah! Would you please? The door is unlocked. He's napping, but don't worry if he wakes up. "

"No problem."

Suniya opened the door and took a look at Mykal's son for the first time since he was born. "Wow, he's a big boy! Mykal, he is so handsome. He looks exactly like you!" She exclaimed as she unbuckled him and took him out of his car seat.

"Thank you." Mykal breathed, speaking to God more so than to Suniya.

Mykal, Jr. immediately stirred. He gave a big yawn and a stretch as he focused on her face. A big smile and a giggle erupted from him as he got a good look at Suniya.

She kissed his chubby cheeks and cooed in his face. "Hey big fella! How are you? You're so handsome! Yes, you are! You look just like daddy! Yes, you do!" Mykal, Jr. loved it. He squirmed and kicked and giggled as Suniya talked to him. "I think he thinks I'm Sissy. He's just as happy as he can be. Look at him giggle."

Mykal came over to her to see. "Well, I doubt it. He hasn't seen Tori since I took him home from the hospital."

"What? She doesn't help you raise him?" Suniya looked shock.

"No! I'm a single dad. Actually, she moved back to Miami! So, it's just the two of us."

"Mykal, I'm so sorry! I had no idea, she left you with the baby to raise alone." Suniya sympathized.

"What? Don't be! This was the deal. Tori didn't want or need a baby. She only had him for me."

"Doesn't she love him?" Suniya stared into Mykal's eyes for an honest response.

"Of course she does, that's why she left him with me. She knows I will take good care of him and give him everything he needs. Sometimes the best thing a mother can do for their baby is to give them to someone who can care for them better than they can. Tori loves him and she misses him, but she knows this is the best thing for him."

"This is so damn sad." Suniya declared, voice choked with emotions.

Mykal caught a glimpse of tears forming in her eyes. He thought her tears were for his son, but he realized they were not. What he said stroke a nerve in her being. Suniya never could understand why Victoria allowed her mother to raise her as her own. Now, it all made perfect since. Victoria was too damaged, too immature and too young to properly raise a child.

"Alright, don't start all that crying. You know I'm sensitive. You'll have my big ass standing out here crying with you." Mykal joked trying to lighten the mood.

It worked. Suniya giggled at the thought. She immediately sucked it up and returned her attention to Mykal, Jr., while Mykal strapped Makayla in the double stroller. Soon they were on their way for a slow leisurely walk in the park.

Pushing the stroller together their hands were only inches apart. It didn't go unnoticed by either of them that their hands were slowly getting closer and closer to each other. As their flesh finally touched an electric spark coursed through their bodies, prompting them to look at each other.

No words needed to be spoken. They didn't need them to communicate. They both new what they wanted, but didn't know how to make it happen.

Fate stepped in one final time as an old couple sitting on a bench spotted them and called them over so they could get a closer look at the babies.

Waving them over with a hand gesture the old lady called out, "Let us see the babies."

They stirred the stroller towards the bench so the couple could get a better look. The senior citizens were so excited they could hardly contain themselves. The man, who walked with a cane watched as his wife got up to get a closer look.

"They're twins, just like I told you Mordechai! One is a boy and the other's a girl."

"Oh! Fraternal twins. How old are they?" The old man inquired as his eyes raked over the seemingly happy family.

Mykal blushed with embarrassment. He never once had to explain that he'd fathered a set of ghetto twins. His eyes widened as he looked to Suniya for an acceptable explanation. He didn't know where to begin to explain his situation to the older couple.

"They're six months old." Suniya offered.

"Ethel, the mother said they're six months old."

"I heard her! I'm standing right next to her! You old fool!" She yelled back to him. "Don't mind him. He can't hear, so he thinks I can't hear either." She giggled. "God bless his soul. Luckily, I love him!"

"What do they look like?" Her husband asked.

"The girl looks just like the mother and the boy looks just like the father." She yelled to him.

"Oh, okay! Beautiful family! You have a beautiful family, so take care of them son. Okay? Y'all stick together, no matter what! Keep your family together, no matter what! Okay? You hear me?"

A lump formed in Mykal's throat. That's all he ever wanted to do. His eyes zoomed in on Suniya's and they pleaded with her to let him do that. Her hands squeezed his tight. "Yes sir! I hear you. I will do my best." Mykal responded as he took Suniya's hand in his and kissed it.

"Good! Well, we've taken up enough of you young folks time. It'll be time to get those young'uns in bed soon. So we'll let you go. Just remember this. A man who want take care of his family is not a man. Do right by that pretty lady. Okay?"

"Yes Sir! I will. I promise." Mykal replied although his eyes never once left Suniya's, as he placed her hand against his heart.

They strolled along in silence for a long time, pondering what just happened. Finally Suniya spoke. "I cooked a big pot of spaghetti. Are you hungry?"

"You know I'm always hungry. Are you inviting me to dinner?" Mykal as puzzled.

"Yeah! Are you coming?" She smiled.

"Sounds like I might be! I hope so, it's been a while! Yeah, definitely think there's a possibility. I can see it in your eyes." Mykal joked.

"You're nasty!" Suniya giggled as she playfully shoved him. "Don't say that in front of the twins."

Mykal, looked at her for a long breath. There was no denying he loved that woman. He had a second chance and he wasn't going to blow it. "I'm going to marry you one day Suniya Simmons and make you the mother of my two children." He declared as their eyes met.

"I'm going to hold you to that promise, Mykal Roman." She replied as she gently sampled his lips. Mykal seal their declaration with a sensual kiss, brief for endearing.

Mykal followed Suniya to her house after they left the park. They had spaghetti for dinner. The following morning they had pancakes for breakfast. The four of them lived together as a family from that moment on.

Mykal kept his word. Six months later Suniya Simmons became Suniya Roman, mother of two.

About Author Brenda Stokes Lee

BRENDA STOKES LEE

Brenda Stokes Lee is an Amazon #1 Bestselling Author in African American, Contemporary and Interracial Romance for her erotic romance novel, Georgia on My Mind. She is also an author, screenwriter, novelist and a good old fashioned storyteller who refuses to let a trivial little thing like the truth come between her and a good story. Born in North Carolina, but raised in the suburbs of Washington D.C., this writer is a Morgan State University graduate who currently resides in Charlotte, North Carolina. Creative, funny and full of tall tales of love, mystery, fantasy, action, intrigue and grown folk's drama, Brenda is determined to make you laugh, to make you cry and most important to make you feel alive.

CONTACT BRENDA

Find Brenda on Facebook

Follow Brenda on Twitter

Brenda's Author's Page

Send Brenda an email

<u>Georgia On My Mind</u>, Amazon #1 Best Selling African American, Contemporary and Interracial Romance Novel.

Georgia Porter is a big, bold, beautiful, black woman who is doing everything hold down her man until he passes the bar. Unfortunately, her man has develop an exit strategy and plans to leave Georgia the moment he gets his bar results. Not only does he plan to leave her, but he plans to marry another woman. Georgia is devastated. Along come a handsome young man from her past who sweeps her off her feet, gets her back in shape and teaches her to love again. Then back crawls the snake who left her. Will Georgia give him another chance? What will she do? Who will she choose? Thick girls get caught up to.

<u>Georgia On My Mind</u> is available on Kindle and Nook.

Unspeakable Proposal, Amazon Best Selling African American, Contemporary and Interracial Romance Novel.

After five years of trying to have a baby, Hope & John Sabin are given bad news. Hope cannot conceive or carry a child. Thirty five years old and desperate, Hope does the unthinkable. She contracts Quanique, a bisexual college student, to have a threesome in hopes of conceiving a child. The trouble with this plan is that Quanique develops some plans of her own and John, Hope's husband is completely unaware that there even is a plan. What would you do? Would you share your marital bed with another woman?

Unspeakable Proposal is available at Amazon and NOOK

<u>Hollywood Strangers</u>, **Amazon** Best Selling African American, Contemporary and Interracial Romance Novel.

Tatyana Fuqua is a beautiful aspiring actress, struggling to break into the Hollywood entertainment industry. The only meaningful relationship she ever had was a platonic one with Lee, her male best friend. Secretly, Tatyana is in love with him. Lee AKA Thomas Malcom Lee, is a handsome LA attorney who has been in love with Tatyana since grade school. He wants to be her man, but Tatyana is hesitant. Tatyana is afraid that if she screws up this relationship, she'd lose her only friend and her safety net in times of trouble. Sadly when she finally gives in to his romantic advances, a misunderstanding rips them apart.

Will they ever find the love their hearts desperately seeks?
Hollywood Strangers, is available on Kindle and Nook.

ABOUT AUTHOR MANSWELL T. PETERSON

MANSWELL T. PETERSON

Manswell T. Peterson has endured many challenges in his life. He decided to put those experiences to good use by writing novels as an adult. In 2007, Peterson debuted with the eye-opener, Am I A Priority In Your Life Or An Option? This was a novel that provides an inside look on the male perspective of juggling women.

Also released in the same year was One Last Cry, which was well received by the reading public. Fascinated with the feedback readers were providing, Manswell penned Love Stories #1 One Last Cry: Confessions of the Other Man in Spring 2008.

Seeing the results of what a man could bring to the literary community, Manswell decided to delve deeper with another persona, Dark Chocolate. Dark's mystery remained cloaked with a logo that kept his online fans wanting more.

Upon the debut of the Cougar Club in 2009, Dark's fans were following his voice with a successful online radio show that captivated hundreds of listeners. Sexy erotica adventures held their attention as they patiently waited for the conclusion.

For the next two years, Manswell decided to work on himself. He ended the radio show and pursued higher education. In the midst of learning, he discovered the love of his life, Dr. Latonya Peterson whom he married. Upon completing his education, Manswell decided to write his memoirs and signed with Nu Cherte Publishing in June 2011. Tracks of My Tears was released June 2012. Tracks of My Tears made him a National Best Selling Author.

Manswell is now founder of his own company Manswell Peterson Studios. He has written other books since 2012 to include(One Last Cry Revisited, One Last Cry: Ron's Revenge, and One Last Cry Remorse, Cougar Club, Cougar Club: Caribbean Getaway, and Man Laws Don't Break'em).

He has written and produced his own movie the "The Mustard Seed" and is working on the pre-production. He is the Department Chair and Instructor of Criminal Justice at Darton State College. He has two sons, Manswell II and Braylen, who are his joy. He is a Disabled Navy Veteran and a proud member of Omega Psi Phi Fraternity.

CONTACT MANSWELL

Twitter: @Manswellp
Facebook: https://www.facebook.com/manswell.peterson
Website: ManswellPeterson.com
E-mail: Manswellp@yahoo.com

ONE LAST CRY REVISITED

Why can't love be easy? Vanessa is married and has it all: rich husband, house, cars, but she is missing something. She is missing the thrill of passion. The chemical and physical romance that two people share can lead to many twists and turns. When you encounter that person, how do you know when not to cross the proverbial line? Could you avoid the pitfall of love, lies, and lust? Follow Vanessa and Ron Williams as their lives are invaded by a stranger named Pete. Watch as the road less traveled can sometimes lead to hurt, then lust, and finally love. The only question is-can they steer clear of the dangers of such a curvy road and get their lives back on track? Or, will they be lost forever in their one last cry?

ONE LAST CRY RON'S REVENGE

Death, divorce, jail, pregnancy, and broken trust -- what a complex and sticky web love and deceit can weave. Part two of this series picks up with everyone adjusting to the changes in their lives since Ron Williams unleashed his fury on that unforgettable night in ER. The death of Pete Sr. continues to weigh heavily on Vanessa's heart as she raises her son, Pete Jr. and nurtures an unlikely friendship. In time, it appears that Vanessa's life is finally turning the corner when a person from her past resurfaces with a secret to tell. Then a car accident threatens a life and reveals a secret that unravels a chain of lies. Lives will be forever changed and rearranged. Ron's revenge will ignite One Last Cry for everyone.

ONE LAST CRY: REMORSE

In love and war, death, divorce, jail, pregnancy, and broken trust -- What a complex and sticky web love and deceit can weave. Part two of this series picks up with everyone adjusting to the changes in their lives since Ron Williams unleashed his fury on that unforgettable night in ER. The death of Pete Sr. continues to weigh heavily on Vanessa's heart as she raises her son, Pete Jr. and nurtures an unlikely friendship. In time, it appears that Vanessa's life is finally turning the corner when a person from her past resurfaces with a secret to tell. Then a car accident threatens a life and reveals a secret that unravels a chain of lies. Lives will be forever changed and rearranged. Ron's revenge will ignite One Last Cry for everyone.